Mike Aleman was born and raised in Chicago but moved to Powder River, Wyoming, when he was 15 years old. He embraced the people of the West and the western way of life immediately and fully, and knows his life was enriched from his experience.

His writing tutorial came from thirty years of teaching high school students the country's best literature and, of course, from reading it from an early age.

Retired, Mike continues to read and write on a daily basis, amazed at the beauty and power of both poetry and prose.

Powder River, 1957 is dedicated to Terry W. Mackey,
a man of Wyoming.

M.P. Aleman

POWDER RIVER, 1957

AUSTIN MACAULEY PUBLISHERS™

LONDON • CAMBRIDGE • NEW YORK • SHARJAH

Ordering Information
Quantity sales: Special discounts are available on quantity purchases by corporations, associations, and others. For details, contact the publisher at the address below.

Publisher's Cataloging-in-Publication data
Aleman, M.P.
Powder River, 1957

ISBN 9798886935912 (Paperback)
ISBN 9798886935929 (Hardback)
ISBN 9798886935936 (ePub e-book)

Library of Congress Control Number: 2023916067

www.austinmacauley.com/us

First Published 2024
Austin Macauley Publishers LLC
40 Wall Street 33rd Floor, Suite 3302
New York, NY 10005
USA

mail-usa@austinmacauley.com
+1 (646) 5125767

I would like to thank Russ Davis for his expertise in putting a manuscript together, and to the folks at Austin Macauley Publishers for their support and vision in making this publication possible.

Also by M. P. Aleman

Cottonwood Springs
The Chalk Dust Poet
Adios Mi Abuela

Chapter One

The day my mother left us, my father found a dog along the highway just outside of Powder River. It had been thrown from a moving car, which at least had the decency to slow down. My father heard the dog yelp as it landed and rolled into the barrow pit. It was lucky he wasn't killed or had any bones broken, so we named him Lucky.

We were living behind Hyatt's General Store in an old, made-over white, wood-frame house. The day we moved in there I found photographs in the basement of German soldiers in bunkers with German shepherd dogs, and always suspected that Hyatt had been a Nazi who'd somehow sneaked into the country after World War II to become a rich general store owner. I never mentioned it to anybody for fear of reprisals. I was only a boy then with an active imagination, in addition to being very unsure of myself.

One thing I was sure of that Saturday morning in April of my 16th year was that my mother was about to leave permanently. My father had gone to work. He was the Postmaster in Powder River, and opened the PO half a day on Saturdays. No sooner had he left the house did she begin packing a suitcase and a denim bag with her belongings. I was barefooted, wearing jeans and a t-shirt, and I stood sipping a cup of coffee, leaning against the door frame of their bedroom, watching her pack.

Lydia was a lithe, pretty, dark-haired woman, thirty-seven years old who harbored dreams of becoming a singer from the time she was young. When they were first married, my father played piano in bars while she sang and shuffled her feet, but as they aged he grew tired of the bar crowd, so they ended their "musical career."

"Don't you love us anymore?" I asked her, my voice sounding foreign and strained.

"I do love you, Matthew," she answered softly, dumping cosmetics, hair curlers and a hand mirror into her denim bag. "I even love Asa in a way, but…"

"But not enough to stay." I finished for her.

"I can't stay. I'm suffocating here. Can't you see that?"

Obviously, I couldn't see it. What I could see was that she recognized only her struggle; and like most adults, she didn't see the problems her actions would create for me or for my father either for that matter. She expected that I should understand her needs when I didn't even know what they were. Besides, my own adolescent needs were raging in my head and behind the scenes, and it was all I could do to understand those.

"Where will you go? Where will you be living? Will I see you anymore?" She straightened up and looked at me, tears in her dark eyes, her hair pulled back in a ponytail, looking not too far removed from the girls I knew at the high school.

"Casper. I'm going to Casper. It's only thirty-eight miles away. I'll see you often. Maybe you can stop by after school some days. We can have dinner."

She was wearing a yellow and red, flowery print dress, white anklets and penny loafers. She held a blue blouse in her hands, kneading it as a cat does a rug. She stood there, her lower lip quivering, her fingers working the blouse.

"Won't you be working?" I asked, blinking back my own tears.

I was aware of a sudden, almost embarrassing adult intimacy between us at that moment; one I'd not felt before. I was being forced into the world of men and women, and even though I was beginning to formulate what it meant to be a man, I wasn't ready for the complexities of the adult world.

"Yes, some, but I'll always have time for you. I've taken a job singing in the lounge at the Gladstone Hotel."

Along with the Townsend Hotel, the Gladstone was one of the two grand hotels in Casper left over from before World War II, when grand hotels of various levels of grandiosity were built near the railroad stations of every city and town from Seattle to New York.

She stuffed the blue blouse in the suitcase and gathered her shoes from the closet floor to shove them down into the bag with her cosmetics. She only had two pair to go with the penny loafers she was wearing.

"You have a boyfriend, don't you?" I asked in an attempt to hurt her, trying to return some of the pain I was feeling. I didn't want to hurt her, not really, but I couldn't understand how she could love me and leave me at the same time. It didn't seem reasonable.

She spun away from the closet and stepped toward me, anger flashing in her eyes. I thought she was going to slap me, and I drew back, but she didn't. She just glared at me, and I felt shameful. I shouldn't have accused her, and I knew it. I looked away. As she went back to her packing she said, "Of course I don't."

"I didn't really think so." I said in weak attempt at an apology.

"If you didn't think so, why did you even suggest it?" she snapped.

"Well, I was sure until this morning that you'd be living here next week, just like always."

I walked over the cold linoleum floor into the kitchen where I poured another cup of coffee. I added milk and sugar, extra sugar this time in an immature act of rebellion and stood at the sink staring at the rusty and green mineral stains. My eyes rose to the window into the prairie beyond.

It was early spring and there was still a thin coating of ice on the watering troughs for the cattle, which stood dumbly across the road from the house with vapor rising from their backs as the sun warmed the frost from their hides. Their brown and white faces stared emptily at me through the window, and I thought how simple and uncomplicated their lives were. They had only to eat and sleep, walk around aimlessly and let their shit drop out along the way until they were ready to be butchered.

I shifted my eyes to the Buick parked in what passed for a driveway. A coating of frost still covered the windshield.

"Are you taking the car?" I called back into the bedroom.

"Yes. You'll still have Asa's pickup. You wouldn't want me to be afoot in Casper, would you?"

I walked back into their bedroom. She was packed and putting on her Sunday coat, a long, dark-blue, wool coat with three big white buttons down the front.

"I don't think it's fair of you to make me tell Asa," I complained.

"I know it isn't, so I left him a note. You can give it to him when he comes home at noon."

"I'm not giving it to him. You do your own dirty work! Stop at the PO why don't you, and give it to him on your way out."

Ignoring my comment, she said, "I'll just put it on the table. Will you carry my bags out to the car for me?"

"No." I said. "If you're going to live alone, you'll have to get used to carrying them yourself."

I drank a big swallow of coffee to keep from sobbing, and almost choked. I had never talked to her like that in my life. I knew she didn't like hearing it, and I didn't like the sound of it myself. Suddenly afraid I was going to faint, I pulled out a chair and sat down at the kitchen table. I'd never before felt faint, and wasn't sure I would, but I certainly felt dizzy, so I put my forehead down on the cold tabletop and closed my eyes.

I heard her lug her bags into the kitchen and out through the back door. I heard the trunk of the Buick slam shut after a few minutes, and then she reentered the kitchen, leaving the door open and allowing the cold morning air to sweep over my bare feet. It revived me and my head cleared instantly. When I lifted my head, she was standing over me with the envelope in her hand. She reached out and leaned it against the sugar bowl.

Suddenly she grabbed me and pulled my head to her breast. I put my arms around her waist and cried into her coat.

"I love you, Matthew. It's not you. It's not even Asa. It's this life. It's the wrong life for me. I don't know how we ended up in Powder River. We just did."

She broke away from me and stepped back.

"I've got to go," she whispered, unable to speak further. "I'll call you." She walked out the kitchen door, pulling it closed quietly behind her.

I sat at the table with my head on my arms, my tears dropping onto the table. I knew it was going to be awful at noon when Asa came home and read her letter. I knew he would ask me why I didn't phone him.

I heard her scraping the frost from the windshield, heard the Buick start. As always, she ground the starter and revved the engine too much. I heard the car drop into gear and listened to the tires on the gravel as she rolled down the driveway from the house to the road. The sound of the car faded as she drove away from the house.

Sitting at the kitchen table in my bare feet I felt too vulnerable, and knowing I didn't want to be around when Asa came home to discover her gone, I dressed, took my bolt-action .22, and a box of bullets. I stuffed two slices of bread and an apple in my jacket pocket and pulled my cowboy hat from the peg on the wall and walked through the same door my mother had just passed through on her way out of my life.

I headed north up the road until I got to the Burlington Northern right-of-way, then followed the tracks west for a mile or two. I approached an overpass, climbed the embankment to the road and stood on the bridge studying the tracks below. I heard the plaintive call of the train whistle and watched as the train came into view. Leaning my rifle against the rail I climbed over the rail, turned and faced the train, my hands holding on to the rail behind me, my boot heels on the edge of the railroad ties that formed the bridge planking. Just before the train reached the overpass, I leaned out, when suddenly the engineer, whose startled face I saw briefly, blew the whistle long and hard, startling me so one hand came free and I started to fall. I twisted around and grabbed the rail with my other hand, hanging desperately while my cowboy hat blew off from the blast of the train passing below me. My feet dangled in the air while I clung to the bridge railing until the train was gone, and I was able to pull myself up and over the rail, where I collapsed onto the bridge and cried until I was all cried out.

Eventually I gathered myself, stood, took the rifle and climbed back down the embankment to retrieve my hat, then continued along the railroad right of way, shooting glass insulators from the telephone poles along the rail bed. I knew it was wrong, knew the sheriff would fine me if he caught me, but it didn't matter to me. It helped me regain a little control over my life, which had been pulled out from under me when my mother drove away from the house.

I shot rabbits too, a couple of jack rabbits and some cotton tails, and left them dead on the plain. Jack rabbits are too tough to eat anyway, and although it was still April and still safe to eat rabbit meat, I didn't want them. I wasn't hunting, I was just killing, and I felt I was shooting rabbits to keep from shooting myself.

I followed the tracks for a while, then cut south-west over Highway 20-26, staying along the riverbed of the South Fork of the Powder River, past the dump down toward Hell's Half Acre. It turned out to be a long walk, but then I needed a long walk, needed to stay away from the house for as long as possible.

The morning sun was warm on my skin, although I could still see my breath as I walked. Even though it was early, the sagebrush and greasewood already had their sweet smell. The frost was beginning to melt, and my boots and cuffs were soaked from walking through the ankle high grass.

The emptiness of the prairie matched my own, but the silence and the vastness made me feel better, and some of my emotion dissipated as I walked. After a while I quit shooting and just slung the .22 over my shoulder, holding it by the barrel, a thing I knew I shouldn't do.

As I walked, my mind worked on the morning's events. Lydia left because she had to leave. She was much more lively than Asa. I could always see that, but in my boyhood innocence I merely enjoyed their contrasting natures. It was always a nice change moving from one to the other; my mother's activity and my father's quiet steadiness.

Asa was really a nice man, and I knew Lydia loved him; and of course, I loved him, loved them both equally, but I liked Asa too. He was a small, mild man who went bald early. I didn't ever know him when he wasn't bald, and I know his baldness bothered my mother.

Asa liked playing the piano, as I said; but he liked studying and reading even more. He was basically a shy man, though he got on well with folks. He liked to talk about the meaning of life and stuff like that, while Lydia wasn't reflective hardly at all. She liked singing and dancing. I know the town's folks thought she was a little odd, for they often saw and heard her singing while dancing as she hung clothes on the line out back.

At sixteen I never thought about the meaning of life or the purpose of human suffering, like Asa sometimes did. None of that came to me until my senior summer, when I caused myself more suffering than I had ever imagined. Before that I lived each day as it came, anticipating the next day in terms of a test, a ballgame or a date.

I had enough to worry about what with trying to figure out how to be with girls, and fitting in at the high school, and doing as well as I could at school work; but I didn't think about life per se. Life was daily living, eating breakfast, going to school and trying to figure out how to speak to adults.

The morning my mother left, however, all I knew turned suddenly unfair. So I walked along the South Fork of the Powder River trying to imagine how Asa and I were going to get along without her.

I stayed out until late afternoon, eating my lunch sitting on the edge of a highway bridge that spanned the river. I tried to puzzle out how a couple could fall in love, get married, have a kid and seem happy, then without warning one of them up and leave on a Saturday morning. I could see though that it was suddenly only to me and Asa, and that Lydia must have been working on it for quite some time.

At that point I realized that Asa had been alone all afternoon with my mother's news in front of him, and I grew worried for him, so hopped down from the bridge rail and headed home.

When I arrived Asa was sitting at the kitchen table, the letter open before him, along with an empty lunch plate and a glass with a film of buttermilk lining its inside. That's the way it was with Asa; no matter the crisis, he could always eat. He could sleep too. I admired his practical tranquility, and later in my life was pleased to have acquired some of it myself.

I stood in the doorway, leaving it open, the temperature having warmed up enough to do so, and we studied each other without speaking. His face was strained and pale, his eyes red-rimmed from the private crying he'd done. He sat hunched over, looking thinner than he really was. I was right to be gone when he got home and read the letter. I removed my jacket and hat and leaned the .22 in the corner.

"Why didn't you call me?" he asked softly.

"I couldn't." I said, taking the chair across from him, turning it backward and straddling it with my arms on the top of the back.

"I don't know. I didn't know what to do. All I could do was get away from here. I needed to be moving, as if putting distance from the house would somehow soften it."

"Are you okay?" I asked him. I wanted to ask him before he asked me. I wanted him to do most of the talking.

"Hell, I don't even know what okay is. Did you ever realize how many times somebody asks you if you're okay, and you say yeah; but okay only means that you're still around, doing what you did before. It don't mean you're at peace or without trouble. It don't mean you're not worried about your job, or that the one you love is in the hospital, or that your wife just left you a note on the kitchen table saying she can't live with you anymore. It only means you haven't died and you're not going to kill yourself. Your heart is broken, but come Monday, you'll go on down and open up the PO and sort the mail and eat your lunch and exchange greeting with folks you've known for years. They'll come in and say, 'Howdy, Asa. How are ya?' and you'll answer, 'Okay.'"

I nodded my understanding, knowing exactly what he meant. "She says here she took a singing job at the Gladstone Hotel."

"Yeah. She told me that."

"Well, she could always sing, that woman. We should have gone down to Denver and let her sing in a big hotel down there. Maybe she'd a got it out of her system. I guess singing at the church ain't enough for her."

"Well I think, Asa, that it is her system. It isn't something she can get out of her. It's just the way she is. What's your system?"

"My system? I guess it's just to be quiet and live without a lot of hullabaloo."

"Will you go after her? Will you talk her into coming back?"

Asa looked at me without speaking, and I could see the wheels turning as to what he might do. He picked up the empty buttermilk glass and looked into it as if it were a crystal ball, then put it to his mouth and drained the remnants. He put the glass down and said, "I need a day or two to think on how to go about it. Maybe she needs a day or two alone. Maybe she'll come back on her own. We'll see."

He rose from the chair and carried his lunch dishes to the sink where he rinsed them and left them. He looked out the window above the sink at the very same scene I looked at a few hours earlier.

"I found a dog," he said so incongruously it took me a few seconds to respond.

"A dog?"

"Yep. Somebody slowed down and threw him out of a car just down from the PO. I was out back and heard it. He's a little red water spaniel of some kind."

"Where is he?" I asked.

"In the back yard."

I rose from the table and walked through the house out the back door to our fenced yard. I saw a small, reddish dog lying in the sun on an old pink rug Asa had put down for it. When I stepped out, it looked up at me, wagging its tail.

"He doesn't bark." Asa said, stepping out behind me.

"What?"

"He doesn't bark. Each time he tries, he coughs a lot like he's got a sore throat."

"A sore throat?" I exclaimed. "I never heard of a dog getting a sore throat."

As if to demonstrate, the dog stood up, lowered its head, stretched out its neck and coughed a hard, rasping cough as if trying to clear its throat.

"What are we going to do with him? Keep him?"

"Just as well," Asa said. "Unless you know somebody who wants him. I don't want to put him down, and I don't feel like driving into Casper to take him to the pound. They'll only shoot him anyway if they can't find him an owner. What do you think?"

"He's a nice dog," I said, kneeling and petting his soft coat as he pushed his wet nose into the palm of my hand and licked my fingers.

"What should we name him?" I asked.

"Well, he's damned lucky he didn't die getting thrown out of the car. Let's call him Lucky."

"Lucky? Come on, Lucky." I said, and the dog's ears perked up and his tail beat a tattoo against my leg.

Every night for a week, Asa sat in his easy chair after dinner, listening to the floor-model Philco radio and rubbing Lucky's throat. It actually made him cough harder; but finally, seven days from the time my mother walked out on us, the dog coughed up a small plastic, gum ball machine charm in the shape of false teeth. It was about the size of my thumbnail, and I wondered how he could breathe, or get any food down at all.

"I'll be damned." Asa said, picking up the charm and examining it.

"That dog's luckier than I thought," I said, which was true enough, though unfortunately not all of his luck would be good luck. But for the time being, it would be good luck that ran with him over the prairie whenever he and I hunted rabbits or walked the lonely roads around Powder River, which we did a lot for a long while after my mother left.

Sunday morning I didn't want to face anyone, so tried to get Asa to let me skip church. I lay in bed while he stood at the door to my room sliding a string tie over his head and adjusting it under the collar of his white shirt.

"Everybody will know." I argued. "I can't face them, Asa, I really can't."

"Sure you can, Matthew. You got to. We can't just roll over and play dead. I feel the same as you, but it's my responsibility to play the piano, and the sooner we face them, the better. If we hide and weep, they'll be knockin on our door wantin to know if we're sick or dead. So get out of that sack and get ready. I don't want to be late."

"You could go alone and tell them I have a cold or something."

"I could, but I won't. I'm not goin to lie to them. Painful as it is, the truth is always best. Besides, I don't want to go alone. I need you with me."

He turned suddenly and left the room, and I knew he'd choked up and couldn't talk. It surprised me that he would have to lean on me just as I was leaning on him, and I felt a little ashamed of myself, so I pushed back the covers and began preparation to run the church gauntlet with him.

I put on newly pressed jeans and white shirt, the last clothes my mother ever ironed for me. Like Asa, I wore a black string tie. While I polished my boots, I thought what I might tell folks when they asked where my mother was. I'd say she'd gone to Casper to be with a sick friend, but then they would ask who the friend was and I'd be up the creek without a paddle.

The church was just a quarter of a mile from our place. It was a one room, wood framed building with plain glass windows and seven pews on each side of a center aisle. The piano sat on the left side of the lectern from which the minister spoke. A knotty pine altar with a wood cross on it was the centerpiece of the sanctuary, made by Riley Mills the year before he rolled his pickup on a Saturday night drunk and died.

A small choir loft that held about nine people sat on the right, and a Bible stand was placed directly in front of the choir. The church didn't have a baptismal font. Whenever a baby was baptized, one of the men held a bowl of regular tap water for the minister to dip his fingers in. I was always disappointed in the tap water, which never seemed holy to me.

For years I told Asa that I was going to build a nice baptismal font, but I never did. I also told Asa that someday I'd buy a nice marble font for the church, with a silver bowl in it and a lid with a cross on the top of it, but I never did that either. Asa reminded me about the road to Hell being paved with good intentions.

The church was heated with electric baseboard heaters along the outer walls of the room. They snapped and popped as they expanded and contracted while heating up or cooling down, often with startling gunshot-like noises that woke even the sleepiest members of the congregation. Baseboard heat didn't seem particularly sacred to me either, and when I complained about it to Asa he asked, "What do you want, a burning bush?"

When we arrived, they already knew Lydia was gone. I have no real idea how they knew, but they did. I suppose Lydia could have let a woman friend know she was going to leave, or she stopped for gas on the way out of town and Ole Anderson read her face, or people saw coming what Asa and I were too close to see.

That's the way it is in a small town. You can't get fined for shooting glass insulators off telephone poles without everyone knowing the exact amount of the fine; and the women always knew the day any of the girls got her first period. You'd a thought Christ himself had come back and made the announcement the way they talked about it.

So as my father and I entered the church, it was clear that everybody knew Lydia was gone. All the women gave me a sympathetic look that wasn't too far removed from the look on their faces the morning their prize bull was going to be slaughtered. People patted Asa's shoulder and whispered condolences, although I couldn't hear what they said to him. To me they said, "Oh, you poor dear," and gave me motherly hugs, pulling me embarrassingly to their matronly breasts.

I had to grind my teeth to get through the service. It made me feel my mother's loss even more than I had the day before, which I didn't think was possible. Seated behind Asa I focused my eyes on the chords of his neck as he played the piano and we all sang, "Bless Be the Tie that Binds." I don't remember hearing one word of the sermon, but it probably wasn't anything special. Reverend Henderson's sermons were never anything special, focusing always on the sinfulness of man or the glory that was God. Variations on those themes filled our Sundays, so that I always looked forward to a guest preacher or a missionary couple from Darkest Africa, which always made me wonder if there was a place called Lighter Africa where the natives were light skinned. The service ended with, "What a Friend We Have in Jesus," but that morning I didn't feel as if Jesus was my friend at all.

I don't know why I didn't just get up and walk out when we sang the words, "…all our sins and griefs to bear." I could bear my own griefs alone, thank you very much. I would have left, I think, except for loyalty to Asa. He played without missing a note, and I figured if he could play his best service the day after his wife walked out of his life, I could sure as hell stay with him.

I wondered how God could let such a thing happen and still expect me to trust in him. If he was such a great and glorious God, why didn't he stop kids from drowning in irrigation ditches, or keep ranch wives from getting cancer, or stop my mother from leaving me?

Chapter Two

After struggling through Sunday, Monday didn't offer any improvement. I had to return to school, for even when family crises occur, you have to go to school, and everybody expects you to be normal, and that day I was anything but normal.

Since Powder River only had a two-room school that took students through the eighth grade, high school students had to ride the school bus into Casper after that.

Natrona County High School, thirty eight miles away, was the closest high school, so every morning at six thirty, an ungodly hour to wait for a school bus, we walked down to the highway, the five or six of us who attended high school, and waited for the bus to pick us up from Waltman, a town twelve miles west of Powder River. Then we'd ride on east on highway 20-26 to Natrona, nine miles toward town and pick up a few more kids, and finally arrive in Casper before eight, just in time for homeroom.

We stood along the highway, our shoulders hunched against the cool morning air, talking or brooding in sleepy silence, sometimes drinking hot coffee from paper cups we'd get from Swede's Shell Service, one of two filling stations in Powder River. In bad weather the Swede let us stand inside. His real name was Ole Andersson, a descendent of one of the thousands of Anderssons who'd emigrated from Norway and Sweden to the Dakotas in the 1800s, and finding the land unforgiving, moved further west to more unforgiving land.

That Monday five of us waited for the bus to arrive: Hetty Place, whose real name was Heather; Tommy Svareland, Adrianna Hudson, me, and Ernie Clapp.

Hetty, like me, was a junior. She was an odd girl, but for good reason. When she was four years old, she got her head stepped on by a horse at a steer roping on her daddy's ranch. Subsequently, Hetty had a horseshoe shaped scar that ran from her cheek up to the temple on the left side of her head, a head shaped more like a melon. Her right eye was a little crooked, shooting off to the right so you couldn't ever tell if she was looking directly at you or not. It took teachers at the high school a few semesters and some embarrassing moments saying, "Hetty, look at me when I'm talking to you," for them to figure it out.

But after Hetty got stepped on, something happened in her brain, or maybe it would have happened anyway, but it seemed she suddenly became a genius in arithmetic. I mean as soon as she started school, her teacher, Rose Schmidt, noticed that Hetty always got all the number problems right, and all the word problems as well. In fact, she shot two years ahead of everybody in the class and stayed there through her senior year of high school.

Hetty was a thin, blond girl, her hair as stiff as hay. She wore thick glasses to compensate for the vision problems she incurred when she got stepped on by that horse. She was a soft-spoken girl, kind, and always helpful to others when they had trouble with confusing arithmetic problems, which always seemed to her, as clear as spring water. The Monday morning after my mother left, Hetty sat next to me on the bus as we rode to school, even though I'd sat way in the back and pretended I was asleep.

It was a cold, clear morning with the sun low in the east as we drove into it. Frost coated the highway except where the traffic had warmed tire-tracks on the road, but you could see heavy frost still on the cars and pickups parked in ranch yards and in front of trailer houses along the route. I looked for antelope, but it was a little early to spot them. By summer the hills would be scattered with small herds and groupings of two or three; and by fall their instincts would tell them it was hunting season and you'd hardly ever see them from the highway.

When the state was dry, which was always, the antelope found their way to the road edge, where any rain run-off would keep the grass green. Lots of antelope became road kill because of grazing along the highway.

I was sitting with my eyes closed when Hetty leaned toward me and whispered, "Matthew, did your Momma go away?"

"Jesus!" I exclaimed. "Does everybody know that?"

"I don't know. My momma told me. She said your mother just up and left Saturday morning and isn't ever coming back. Is that so?"

"I don't know if she's coming back or not, Hetty."

"Well, I'm sorry she went. I know how I'd feel if my momma left me. I'd feel just awful. I'd probably die."

"Yeah, well, I'd rather not talk about it, if you don't mind, Hetty."

"I know," she said. "I wouldn't want to talk about it either, but I want you to know, Matthew, that I'm your true friend in this, and I didn't mean to make you feel bad."

"Thank you, but I already felt bad, and I think I'm going to feel bad for a long time, but you didn't do it, so don't worry about it."

It was a relief to get to school and get to class, because most of my classmates didn't live in Powder River and didn't know about my mother, so I drifted through the school day in reasonable order, not participating much, but still answering questions when called upon. So the day passed uneventfully and slowly, until we were standing around after school waiting for the bus to pick us up for the long ride home.

Generally I was not a trouble maker, and avoided trouble purposefully, but that day I was certainly looking for it. And did you ever notice that when your life goes to hell, how willing you are to go right along with it? As I've said, Hetty looked odd, but we who grew up with her didn't notice much; and we never made fun of her because from the day she returned after her accident, the two Powder River school teachers made it clear that we'd catch hell if we ever teased her or were unkind. But it wasn't fear of adult wrath that kept us from it. Hetty was one of us, we liked her, and all of our parents were friends. No one ever imagined being unkind to her, but with the town kids, it was a different story.

That afternoon we were waiting for the school bus in front of the high school on the corner of Ninth and Elm. Our bus always came a little later than the town busses, and we were standing around on the lawn; Hetty and Adriana together, and Ernie, Tommy and I in a group a few yards away when a couple of jocks interfered with Betty. Looking back I can see it was just teasing, could even see it then, but I didn't care. I was in no mood for teasing, and I stepped in without thinking too much about it.

Four boys wearing orange and black lettermen jackets strolled past. Two of them were big guys, football players, and as they passed Hetty, one of them, a big, red-headed guy, reached out and pulled the books from her arms, sending them to the sidewalk. Kids always did that. Normally you just swore at them or flipped them off, but Hetty didn't answer. She just picked up her books and glared at them until one of them called out, "Four-eyes," and another made a comment about her being a Flat Head Indian.

"Hey!" I shouted, dropping my books and stepping up to them. "Don't you ever bother her!"

"What are you, her father?" Red asked through a nasty grin.

"You two go together, do you?" he sneered, making his companions laugh.

"Listen," I said. "You don't understand, so just leave her alone."

We were all in a distorted circle now, Red and his cronies one half of it, they just back of him, their chests puffed out, their shoulders squared. The Powder River kids made up the other half of the circle, with me out front, nervous tension making my right leg quiver.

"It's all right, Matthew," Hetty said, trying to diffuse that which couldn't be diffused, that which had been set in motion Saturday morning.

"It was just my books."

"Yeah, it was just her books, shit kicker; just her four-eyed, flat-headed books."

I hit him a good left hand in the nose and kneed him in the balls; and when he went down, I kicked him for good measure. His pals were all over me in a flash, and I felt my left eyebrow split. I was down then too, and tried to cover up as they kicked at me and punched me, and I could hear kids screaming, "Fight! Fight!"

Hetty's voice called out, "Oh no, Matthew! No Matthew!"

I kept trying to cover up, felt kicks in my back, and I could hear Tommy Svareland's voice getting higher and higher as his excitement grew, yelling, "You sons a bitches! You dirty sons of bitches!"

Finally two teachers got there and broke the whole thing up. We all sat in the principal's office, the combatants holding ice packs over our bruises and open wounds. No real damage had been done. Red's nose was not broken, although I don't know why. I'd certainly hit him hard enough. My eyebrow didn't need stitches either. So we sat there hearing the principal lecture all of us; the country kids and the city kids telling their side of the story, until we were forced to shake hands and apologize, hating every minute of it and meaning none of it. Red and I got suspended for three days, which was all right with me, since I wasn't in much of a mood for school that week anyway. The ride to Powder River was long and silent, as the bus driver was mad as hell that he had to wait his dinner because of our shenanigans.

"You should have known better," Asa said that evening sitting across from me at the kitchen table, still wearing his blue Postmaster baseball cap on the back of his bald head.

"I knew better." I confessed.

"So, how's your eyebrow? Gonna need stitches?"

"No. The school nurse pinched it together and taped it. Hurt more than when he hit me."

"You hurt anywhere else?" I hurt in my heart, but I didn't tell him that. He knew it anyway.

"Just bruised. My back hurts some, and I'm feeling stiff, but I'll be okay."

"I'll run you an Epsom Salts bath after dinner. It'll help take some of the hurt out."

He paused, studying my eyes closely and asked, "Are you really going to be okay? I mean you can't go around mad at the world when it's really Lydia you're mad at."

"I know. I'll be okay. How about you?"

"Same as you," he assured me. "Same as you."

Asa fixed fried pork chops and fried potatoes, green beans, bread and applesauce. We lingered over the meal, reluctant to get away from the table and sit in the living room without Lydia there. I ignored my school work and read from a western paperback novel called, Gunman's Revenge.

Asa read the Rocky Mountain News. Lucky sat with his head resting on Asa's stocking feet.

As I stood to get ready for bed, Asa said, "You can work with me at the PO these next three days. I'll pay you a dollar and a quarter an hour. I expect you can use the money, and I could use a little company down there right now. It'll be good not to be alone for a couple days. Good night now."

"Good night, Asa," I said, heading out of the room. "And thanks."

The next day Asa closed the P.O. early and drove alone into Casper to see if he could get my mother to return, but she wouldn't even let him in her apartment, standing at the door with it slightly open, as if guarding the place from intruders. He offered to ask the PO to transfer him into Casper, offered to quit his job altogether and move to Denver where she could sing in a big hotel; but she would have none of it, and he returned with his already broken heart completely dispirited.

"It makes no sense to me," he said. "No sense at all. I'm afraid the woman has gone crazy. That's the only explanation."

Every time Asa went in to Casper he tried again, always returning frustrated and pained, until finally he gave up on it. And so we began our life alone, adjusting each day to our new situation, learning to depend on one another where once we'd depended on Lydia.

Chapter Three

By mid-May my father and I had acquired the routine necessary to make it look as if we could survive very well without Lydia. The town's people were certain we'd adapted. It was easy for them to write Lydia off, for them it was good gossip, and because Asa went to work daily and I returned to my more normal behavior at school, it was apparent to them that Asa and I were strong of character, and that God had given us the courage to accept life's tests bravely.

But we deceived them. We cried alone in our beds, or tears would run freely from my eyes while I was walking the prairie with Lucky, his nose to the ground in search of rabbits as he ran ahead of me. Asa too, took long, solitary walks in the country surrounding Powder River, a thing he hadn't done before.

We cooked our meals routinely, but only ate a portion of them for the first month after my mother's departure. Meanwhile, the dog got fat on leftovers. We kept a clean house after a fashion, often waiting until there wasn't a clean sock or a clean pair of shorts between us before doing our laundry. We did the dishes when there weren't any left to use, and we didn't make a bed for months. But we went to work and school, and Asa played piano on Sundays with me sitting faithfully behind him. In short, we survived.

Fortunately, life in Powder River distracted us from our own problems, as we became aware of other aspects in the lives of the people around us.

Herb and Rose Schmidt, a strait-laced, dedicated couple, were our teachers at the Powder River school, a two room, white framed structure trimmed in green. It had living quarters in the back of the classrooms for its resident teachers.

In addition to teaching, Herb Schmidt could play a mean fiddle. In fact, he was one of the finest fiddlers in Wyoming at the time, and played regularly at dances and county fairs throughout the state from Cheyenne to Jackson Hole.

Saturday night, May 17th, there was a dance at the American Legion Hall. Herb fiddled. Folks danced and drank, not necessarily in equal amounts. A rancher punched his wife in the nose and she had to be driven to Casper to get it packed. Clara Moody's new father-in-law, eighty-seven years old, threw up on the dance floor, causing a twenty-minute delay for clean-up. It was a typical Powder River dance.

Then, according to Asa, for I'd left the dance hall by ten, at about eleven-thirty, Herb took one of his infrequent breaks and walked into the bar to order his usual ginger ale. Herb was a one hundred percent teetotaler. Everybody knew that, and although they kidded him about it from time to time, that Saturday night it finally got out of hand.

Apparently Herb was leaning against the bar sipping his ginger ale when a bunch of drunk cowboys and REA workers began to bait him about not drinking. The Rural

Electric Association was stringing wire across the center of the state in those days, and work crews lived for weeks at a time in motels and cabins in the towns that dotted the highway: Natrona, Powder River, Hiland, Moneta, places like that, some of which have since disappeared from the map.

Anyway, one of the Powder River crew offered to buy Herb a "real drink." Herb refused politely, as was his way.

"Come on. Come on! One little drink, Herb. It ain't gonna hurt you. My father told me never to trust a man who wouldn't drink with me."

"Your father didn't know me," Herb stated evenly.

The REA crewman grew irritated at Herb's refusal, so continued his challenge, and it wasn't long before the rest of his boys were in on it, badgering Herb to take just one drink to show that, "we're all friends here."

Herb didn't like having to prove his friendship. He thought he'd established his friendship a long time ago; after all, Herb and Rose had taught all of the children in Powder River for years. But, of course, the REA crew member wasn't a local, he was just passing through, so persisted in his efforts to get Herb to drink with him.

I figured the Powder River ranchers and cowboys would have defended Herb. They knew he wasn't a man for alcohol, that he meant no offense by not drinking with them. Maybe it happened too fast. Maybe they didn't realize the seriousness of the situation, having kidded Herb themselves a little over the years. Or maybe they had always resented Herb not drinking with them and so it rose to the surface that night. Who really knows what goes on in the human mind? Wherever it originated, in the haze of drink and the excitement of the challenge, a few of them began to join in, especially after an unnamed cowboy put five silver dollars on the bar and called out, "Herb, if you drink one single shot, them dollars are yours, all five of 'em." Others took up the cry, adding to the challenge by stacking silver dollars on the bar until there must have been over a hundred dollars stacked up neatly for everyone to see. With so much silver winking in the lights of the bar just waiting for Herb to claim it, the crowd began to chant, "Drink it! Drink it," all the while clapping their hands in time to their chanting until it sounded like a rally in prewar Germany. Maybe what Herb did was because he was an old German named Schmidt who'd abhorred what Hitler did to Germany in the thirties and forties, the chanting got to him. He'd certainly taught us the horror of it when we sat before him in class. Maybe it was the realization that so many of his friends didn't really respect his teetotaling; but when an anonymous voice from the back of the pack called out, "Come on, Herb! You ain't got a hair on your ass if you don't pick up that drink." He picked up the shot glass, and without a word hurled it into the mirror behind the bar, sending cracks out from the point of impact like fingers of lightning. First a collective gasp followed by silence, then Herb, with great dignity walked out of the bar to the dance hall, snapped his fiddle case closed and walked out of the American Legion Hall for the last time.

That very night, with everybody grumbling in their beds about Herb being such a poor loser, he and Rose packed their belongings in their new, 1956 Chevy pickup and the six-foot trailer he used for hauling garbage, and drove away into the night. They never even collected their last month's wages, which lead to rumors that they had hoarded every penny they ever earned.

I was sitting up in bed the next morning while Asa stood at my bedroom door giving me the news. I was shocked at their behavior, and filled with righteous indignation I asked, "How can people be so stupid? He was their friend. He was the best teacher I ever had, and the only teacher most of us had until we went to the high school. Those dumb bastards!"

I was nearly in tears. The event came too closely on the heels of my mother's departure, and I felt my world was coming apart. In April I'd learned that those reliable figures who had inhabited my days could be gone without a moment's notice, and Herb and Rose's action only supported that.

"You might keep in mind," Asa responded, "that those dumb bastards are your people, your friends."

"They're no people of mine. Friends? They were Herb's friends too until last night, and they drove him out."

"Perhaps they did," Asa said, standing in front of the living room mirror combing his bald head, a thing he always did which I never understood.

"It was surely thoughtless of them, I agree; but Herb made the decision to move away. I don't find fault in him for wanting to leave, but I don't think he did it right. He should have given notice, should have finished out his contract and not let his students down because of anger and damaged pride."

Personally I was proud of Herb's actions. To quit, to walk away without looking back was a thing a kid thought admirable. To every one of us kids, for a while anyway, Herb was the only worthwhile man in the bunch.

"Those folks last night were infantile in their behavior, I'll grant you that." Asa continued. "They all knew better, but it was the whiskey talkin, and they'll regret it this morning."

"Regret won't get our teacher back," I countered. "Besides, if you can excuse them, you have to excuse Herb too."

"I suppose you're right." Asa conceded. "But what's done is done, and we've got to move on."

He turned away and began to leave the room when I called him back. "Asa?"

"Yes?"

"Lydia's gone and left us, and now my teachers are gone too. You wouldn't leave for any reason, would you?"

He came to my bed and put his hand reassuringly on my shoulder. "You can count on me, Matthew. I'm not going anywhere. We got to count on each other now, don't we?"

Tears welled up in my eyes, and I could only nod.

"Let's get ready for church. The best thing we can do is keep on keeping on like always."

Since the first Sunday I attended church without Lydia, it had become a burden far greater than I imagined it would be. Until then it had been a comfort, a place of love and support, a place I could count on. Now, not only did I have to sit there without my mother, I had to sit among hypocrites. I looked at each face as folks filed in, searching for clear evidence of guilt, but I found it in only a few; and I realized that most of the people at the Legion Hall who had baited Herb in their drunkenness were REA men and cowboys who didn't live in Powder River, whose kids, if any, didn't attend the Powder River school. They were men who came to town to drink and dance, get laid, and get their pickups greased and gassed up at Swede's Shell Service. The guilt I did see on the few faces which revealed it, was there because they hadn't defended Herb when they had the chance. I knew Asa was right. What I saw on their faces that grim Sunday morning was regret and shame. They'd let a friend down, and they wished they had done better.

But I was hard on them in the early days of that summer. I was unforgiving because I hadn't yet learned my own sin, seen my own flaws, and didn't know how powerful they are in determining personal behavior. In my self-righteousness, I knew I'd never let a friend down as easily as they had done.

The sermon that morning was another of the Reverend Henderson's finger-pointing harangues on man's sinful nature; delivered deliberately and off the cuff on the special occasion of Herb and Rose's departure, and pointed specifically to those who had failed a friend in need. He got so vile and unforgiving himself, that by the time he was finished, I felt sorry for the townspeople and angry at the reverend for taking advantage of their vulnerability. But he had a captive audience and the opportunity, and it was clear that he didn't want it to slip away.

Reverend Henderson's prayers were for Herb and Rose as they entered a new phase of their lives; and I was struck with the fact that no one prayed for my mother the day after she left. We also prayed for forgiveness, guidance and strength to be better human beings, better representatives of Christ on earth.

All in all I found the weekend mentally and emotionally exhausting, and was happy to board the bus for our return to school on Monday morning, where the major issue was clearer, if not any easier. Who was I going to ask to the Junior/Senior prom the first week of June?

I was a poor dater, and had a reputation for being a poor date. I had had a couple of dates as a sophomore, but they were truly miserable failures. For the first one I asked a classmate named Jenny Carstairs, whom the boys referred to as Miss Carnation Milk because she had the biggest breasts we'd ever hoped to bury our faces between. With sweaty palms and butterflies in my stomach, we stepped out on the dance floor with dozens of others just as Elvis Presley began the throbbing rhythm of, "Don't Be Cruel." The floor filled with hips, elbows, bouncing breasts and butts bumping whatever got in the way. We were doing well, albeit self-consciously, right along with the rest when for no explainable reason we both crashed to the floor.

Jenny was wearing a felt, A-line skirt, and her legs shot straight up, revealing chunky thighs and pink panties. The spectators around us let out a collective gasp, followed immediately by unabashed laughter. With a red face and the butterflies in my stomach replaced by a slick coat of shame, I got up and pulled Jenny to her feet, too embarrassed to laugh it off, while she, of course, giggled hysterically. The evening was over for me, and I waited until January to try again.

My second sophomore dating disaster was with a girl named Bobbie Crumly. We went to a western movie, which I loved. The 3:10 to Yuma starred Glenn Ford and Van Heflin, background music sung by Frankie Lane.

She grew sullen and quiet, so in the car afterwards, I looked for a way to change the topic of conversation away from the movie. I had noticed that Jenny's nose was crooked, with a lump on each side. I reasonably assumed she had broken her nose at some point in her childhood; and having heard that girls liked to talk about themselves, I asked with great interest.

"How did you break your nose Jenny?"

Her head snapped around so fast her eyes clicked, and the look in them told me my error even before she whispered indignantly, "I never broke my nose. I want to go home. Take me home now!"

I would rather she'd shouted it or demanded an apology, as her whisper frightened me. So I drove her home. When we pulled up to her house, even before the car came to a full stop, she had the door open and was out of the car. She slammed the door of the Buick so hard I feared she'd cracked the window.

"Don't bother to call me!" She hissed.

Such was the beginning of my dating experiences, so it was with great reluctance that I thought about the upcoming Junior-Senior Prom. To add to my apprehension, it was a formal dance, my first. It meant dinner and flowers. Would I have to pin the corsage on her breast? I was truly worried. And, of course, the whole thing could cost me as much as fifteen bucks.

So what I did pretty much what I'd always done. I played it safe. I asked Hetty. It was easy to do. We'd been friends so long we felt comfortable with one another; and knowing it was Hetty's first date ever, I felt on solid ground.

I was aware that she'd not get asked if I didn't ask her, but it wasn't because I felt sorry for her. It was just the easiest thing to do, is all.

She was aware of it too, of course. The day I asked her, and I remember every detail of it, we were riding home from school on that interminably long, thirty-eight-mile bus trip. The sun was unusually hot for that time of year. Hetty was wearing her hair soft around her face, and loose in a futile attempt to cover up the flatness of her head. She never wore a pony tail, for example, which was the rage then. Her pink-rimmed, Coke-bottle thick glasses rested heavily on her nose. She had on a white blouse and a dark skirt, which was what all the girls at Natrona County High had to wear as a uniform. She had on a light, opened sweater over her blouse, and brown and white saddle shoes. I remember thinking her legs were pretty thin. She was fairly small breasted, and I wondered how she'd keep up a strapless formal dress. Were all formal gowns strapless? I didn't know. Anyway, when I asked her, she looked at me without smiling and said, "Oh Matthew, you don't have to do that."

"Do what?" As if I didn't know.

"Ask me to the prom. You don't have to do it."

"Hetty, I wouldn't ask if I didn't want to take you. You've known me long enough to know I wouldn't do a thing like that."

"Matthew, I know what I look like; and you know what my coordination is like. Since I was four years old, I haven't been able to run straight without falling down, much less dance."

"Hetty, it's our Junior-Senior prom. We should go. We'll have a nice time. We don't even have to dance if you don't want to."

"Well, we couldn't dance the fast ones. I'd fall down for sure, but you'd be holding me for the slow ones, so maybe it would be okay."

"Hell, I fell down last year and I've never even been stepped on by a horse," I said, laughing; and she found it pretty funny herself.

"If we go," she began, as the bus stopped to let the Natrona kids off. "If we go, I don't want you to think we have to go steady or anything. I know that's how boys think; that if they take a girl to the prom, she'll feel it's the beginning of going steady. I don't want you to feel that way."

"I know," I assured her. "We'll just go to dinner and then to the dance."

She was right. Guys did think that way, and many of the guys I knew wouldn't even ask a girl to a prom because they were afraid everybody would think they were going steady. I felt the pressure a little myself, but I knew she was being honest with me, so those thoughts didn't last long.

The night before the prom, Hetty's dad, Ralph, came to our house and offered his Cadillac for the next night. He was, like so many ranchers I knew, big in the belly and skinny in the butt. I think it's because they ride horses until they can no longer ride due to arthritis or general stiffness in their hips, then they sit in pickups; but never so much as walk from a bunkhouse to a corral. To the cowboy there was something shameful about being afoot. Sitting astride a horse gave a cowboy dignity that a farmer just didn't have.

So Mr. Place stood in our living room, his belly hiding his silver dollar belt buckle, offering me his Cadillac.

"If you wash the mud and the manure off it, you can take it," he said. Then he took a wad of bills that would choke a horse from his shirt pocket, and tried to give me fifty bucks.

"You been kind to Hetty, Matthew, sticking up for her at school and all. I'd like to repay you for your kindness."

I refused the offer, which Asa said was the wisest thing I ever did; and considering what happened later in the summer, he was right.

"I appreciate it, Mr. Place, I really do, but it wouldn't be any good that way. If I don't pay for the prom, it wouldn't be mine. The Cadillac is okay, it'll make it special, but I can't take the money. Hetty and I have been friends a long time, Mr. Place. I haven't done anything for her because I feel sorry for her or anything. People shouldn't have to pay their friends for stuff they do. Besides, I don't think Hetty would like it."

He was reluctant to let me have my way, but finally folded the fifty-dollar bill in with the rest of the wad and stuffed it back in his pocket.

"I suppose you're right," he said. "You're a good boy, Matthew, and if you ever need a favor, you let me know. You been a good friend to Hetty, and I won't forget it."

The next morning I drove the pickup over to Place's ranch, where Hetty and I washed the Cadillac. We got more water on one another than we did on the car, but we had a good time. The Cadillac was cream colored, with white-walled tires. It was just about the longest and widest car I'd ever seen.

When I picked her up that night, she looked nicer than ever before. Her momma had taken her in to Casper and had her hair curled and teased out in a way that made her head look almost round. She wore it that way the whole next year. It's a wonder they didn't think of it before.

Her dress was light blue, with a short cape to go over her shoulders. She didn't exactly look beautiful, but she looked pretty in an innocent, fresh sort of way, kind of like a lamb a week after it's been born. Mrs. Place pinned Hetty's corsage on for me, and they took pictures as if it were the last time in their lives they would have the opportunity to do so.

I rented a white sport coat and black pants for the occasion. Marty Robbins was singing, A White Sport Coat and a Pink Carnation, on the radio then, and every guy had to have one. There were more white sport coats at the prom than I'd ever seen in my life.

I couldn't make myself wear black, patent leather shoes though, so I put a high shine on my black cowboy boots and wore those. Hetty bought me a carnation for my lapel, and her mother pinned that on as well. After the dance I put it on a shelf in the back of the refrigerator, where it sat for a year growing ever more wilted and tight, until it looked like a wrinkled, baby fist.

We ate dinner at the Riverside Club in North Casper, which sat right on the North Platte River. We each had a steak and a baked potato with bacon bits and chives on it. I was relieved that nothing disastrous happened as it so often can at prom-night dinners. I didn't spill any food on my clothes or burp suddenly or anything like that, but I was relieved when the dinner was over and we headed to the dance.

The dance, held at the school gym was decorated with twisted, crepe paper streamers in spring colors, and the lunch room tables were covered with white table cloths. Hetty and I danced a few slow ones, and it was nice holding her and being close to her. We didn't try any fast dances, but were content to watch others dance. Ernie Clapp and Adriana Hudson shared a table with us and a number of kids we knew by sight stopped by and everyone said how nice everyone else looked.

Hetty's folks wanted her home at midnight, so we left the school at eleven, but decided to drive up to Casper Mountain and park on the road that leads to Bear Trap Meadow. We sat side by side on that wide front seat mostly talking, but touching and kissing one another tentatively, pretending for a while that we were in love with one another.

I had her home at two o'clock, but nobody ever mentioned it. I drove home afterwards feeling at once noble for taking Hetty, and guilty for the bit of petting to which I'd obviously introduced her.

Monday, however, when we boarded the bus for school, everything was back to normal. While we waited for the school bus to arrive, Hetty and I spoke about what a good time we had, then sat with other friends and established that we weren't going steady. On the ride home we sat together again, and it was like old times. After that we didn't necessarily spend more time with one another than we had before, but we didn't spend any less time either, and she continued to help me with my math, until summer that is, when everything changed anyway.

Chapter Four

My school year ended uneventfully. We got out of school at noon on June 10th, and I walked over to visit with my mother for the afternoon. I'd been there twice before, but was uncomfortable there, and still terribly unsettled about her leaving.

She was living in a small, one-bedroom apartment at 8th and Wolcott, just across the street from the Presbyterian Church. Her apartment faced a park, and I was pleased that she was living in a nice place with a little bit of space around it with a pleasant view.

Our visit was stiff and uncomfortable, but she did seem interested in the news from Powder River, disturbed that Rose and Herb Schmidt were gone, but happy with my account of prom night.

Lydia appeared to be more alive in her new life than she had been in the last years of her previous one with us. She was singing six nights a week at the Gladstone Hotel, sleeping late mornings, and practicing old and new songs in the afternoons. She was also taking voice lessons. She had also bought new dresses and gowns for her work, and pulled them proudly from her closet to show them off for me. They were far removed from the flowered, print dresses she had worn in Powder River. They had sequins, slits up the leg, and were fairly low cut, so I was glad she didn't model them for me. They seemed very expensive to me, and I resented them without knowing why.

"Do you like this one?" she asked, holding a red and black gown in front of her and swirling around a bit.

"It doesn't look like you," I offered, uncomfortably. My comment disappointed her, and she didn't hold up another.

"I've got new perfume too," she said, holding up a tiny bottle with a spray bulb on the top. She shot a little into the air.

"Isn't it fragrant?"

"You didn't use to wear perfume in Powder River," I said, immediately regretting my words. She put the bottle down, and without saying more, hung the gowns in her closet.

Suddenly we had nothing further to say to one another, so I got up to go, and she expressed her desire to walk me down to the bus depot on Center Street next to the court house. She insisted on paying the three dollars for my ticket.

She hugged me and kissed me just before I boarded. I clung to her momentarily, aware of the scent of the perfume I'd criticized just a few moments before. It was nice perfume, not too flowery, and I did like it, but she no longer smelled like the mother I'd known earlier, and I realized painfully that she really was no longer that mother. She wasn't a stranger by any means, but she was different, somehow happier, and I struggled with the knowledge that she'd been so unhappy while she was living with me.

"Give Asa my regards," she said, with sadness in her eyes. "I will," I promised.

We stood for a moment, the Trailways bus idling just behind us. "Won't you come home?" I asked unexpectedly.

"I can't. You must see that."

I nodded, then turned and boarded the bus. I took a window seat and looked out at her, a little choked up and trying to look brave. She too smiled through her tears, and waved to me as the bus pulled away.

As I rode alone on the journey homeward, past the tank farms, tool companies and other oil-related businesses, I wondered at the world of adults, which seemed confusing and unclear. I didn't understand how you could love someone enough to marry them, and then somewhere along the line not love them anymore; or maybe love them, but not enough to stay. My mother and Asa were good people. Why didn't it work for them? Was it that she changed over the years and he didn't? Or was he a way she didn't realize in the early years, and so became disappointed in him later? Or did they just get married because it was what people did in those days, expecting somehow to live happily ever after, like in the storybooks of their youth? I thought I probably wouldn't marry, wouldn't risk causing and feeling again the suffering Asa and I were going through. I was sure there'd be enough of it without me adding to it out of foolishness or error. Apparently my mother had made a serious error in marrying Asa before she really knew what she wanted out of life.

So I rode home to my summer vacation, one which I would be called upon to write about in my senior English class in the fall, just as I had been asked to do every year since I could remember, but one that I would just as soon forget!

Until that summer, vacations had been spent with Tommy Svareland, hunting rabbits, shooting tin cans and exploring the countryside around Powder River. Tommy's mother had died in childbirth, and he lived with his grandmother Svareland and his father, Clive. Clive was a poacher, and everybody knew it. He'd been fined plenty, but it didn't deter him. It's what he was. Asa was the Postmaster. Clive was the resident poacher.

He was a giant of a man, standing six foot eight. I never knew what he weighed, but it was considerable. According to Asa, Clive was also a coward and a bully, beating up on smaller men, or men who'd had too much to drink and couldn't defend themselves; but he ran from a fight with men tough enough to whip him. Most men didn't like him, but it was different with the women, because Clive was a handsome devil, and terribly nice to children. It was amazing how many times he kept one of the Powder River kids from harm. He always seemed to be the one around when a kid was in trouble, probably because he didn't work all that much. For example, he was at the head of the search party three years before when the two Shugart brothers got lost in a snowstorm on their winter range. It was Clive who stayed out long after the Sheriff's search party had quit for the night, until he found the boys frightened and freezing and brought them home safely. He'd also saved Lilly Carlyle from drowning in an irrigation ditch when she was seven, and removed more slivers from kids than most mothers had done themselves. Subsequently, the town put up with him.

The first and only time I hunted with him, we poached. I didn't know we were going hunting, much less poaching.

Probably, Clive didn't know it either. He told Asa he was going to drive out and look at some cattle he was thinking of buying and fattening up to sell, and asked if I wanted to ride along with him and Tommy. Although he should have known better, Asa didn't see any harm in it, so that morning, Tommy, Clive and I rode in his Dodge pickup along one of the dirt roads leading out of Powder River. Clive always kept a lever action 30-30 in the gun rack of his truck, and we hadn't been on the road ten minutes when he spotted six pronghorn antelope grazing along the hillside.

"Jesus, will you take a look at that!" He said excitedly, as he brought the truck to a sliding halt in the middle of the road.

"Fresh meat. You boys slide over."

He took the rifle from the gun rack pointing it out the open window and jacked a shell into the chamber, an awkward feat with three of us packed in the cab of the pickup. He sighted in on the antelope, the rifle resting on the door of the driver's side. The antelope, about sixty yards from the road, turned their heads to observe the stopped vehicle. Clive fired once. I went temporarily deaf as the concussion jolted the cab, the sound reverberating around us. I saw a young buck go down, then spring up again and streak away after the others which had bolted at the sound of the rifle fire.

It's illegal to hunt out of season, illegal to shoot from a vehicle, and illegal to shoot across a country road, but Clive wasn't about to let a few legalities stop him from getting his meat.

"Hold this," he said, handing the rifle to Tommy. Then Clive leapt from the truck, ran to the barbed wire fence, and taking a small pair of wire cutters from his hip pocket, snipped the three strands of wire. Of course, it's long been illegal to cut a fence; and years ago they branded or shot any man who did so, but it seemed perfectly natural to Clive.

He was back in the pickup in a flash, throwing the truck in gear, sending us barreling across the open prairie, bouncing high and hard against the interior of the pickup. It was like bronc riding, both frightening and exhilarating at once, and I hung on for dear life, my eyes wide, laughing and whooping it up right along with Clive and Tommy, who'd been through it so many times that they knew the footholds and handholds which kept them from the bruises I incurred.

Even though I knew it was wrong, I loved the adventure. Clive Svareland had a cavalier attitude about him that a young boy couldn't resist. He was a likable rogue in contrast to the rest of our fathers, who lived by the rules and worked hard to receive the rewards they sought. Clive's rewards were simpler and fewer, but more immediate, and a hell of a lot more fun; or so it seemed to me until I grew old enough to reason more clearly.

He didn't get his antelope that day, however. Even wounded, it went over another fence that Clive would have been happy to cut as well, but for some cattle trucks on the horizon and two horsemen working the cattle who paused in their work to study us as we bounced along.

"Let's get the hell outta here," Clive shouted when he sighted the cowboys, and we turned and headed back even faster than we'd gone in.

When in my eagerness to share my good time I told Asa about the morning, he was furious. Seldom did I see him that angry. Generally, Asa was a man of strong, quiet character and courage. He instructed me never again to ride with Clive; and that evening he walked up to Clive's place and told him that if he ever took me along on another poaching trip he'd haul him in to the game warden personally. Being the coward that he was, Clive swore to the agreement, and I was never again invited. From time to time I stood enviously at the side of the road and watched Clive and Tommy streak off in search of wild game.

Until the summer I was sixteen, Tommy and I were almost inseparable. Even in early June of that year we spent time together. He was young for a sophomore, and I was sixteen, though my mother's leaving was making me older than my years. Still for a while, Tommy's presence was a comfort, and we scouted around as boys will before they begin to compete seriously for an overblown sense of dominance.

Just after school was out, Tommy and I were rabbit hunting near the Powder River dump with Lucky running ahead of us, his nose to the ground trying to pick up whatever scent he could sniff out. He wasn't much of a hunting dog, however, as he was too undisciplined, and his excited barking flushed rabbits so far ahead of us we could never get a decent shot. I learned early that if we wanted to do serious hunting, I had to leave him home, but a boy's hunting is often so much talking and walking anyway, so we were pretty content just being out of school with the freedom to roam at will.

The Powder River dump wasn't what anyone would call a landfill. It was just a series of gullies and washes where we dumped the trash we didn't burn in a fifty-gallon drum.

Old cars dotted the area like dinosaurs gone to die, and odd sculptures of cast-aside stoves and refrigerators, empty wire spools, sofas, tires, car seats and what-have-you, cluttered the countryside. We'd been out about an hour-and-a-half when Lucky ran the end of a coil of barbed wire through his eyelid. We heard him cry out and saw him pull back, skittering around while trying to get free.

"Look! He's tearing his eye out! He's tearing it out!" Tommy cried out as we neared the dog.

"Grab him!" I shouted, dropping my .22 and pouncing on Lucky to keep him from doing even more damage. His yelping scared us, making the crisis even more horrible than it really was.

I held him tightly in my arms, trying to keep his head from thrashing around in his attempts to pull free from the wire. It was the end of a long coil, twenty or so feet, lying in high sagebrush and grease wood so he didn't see it. He'd run the end of the wire into his eyelid and out again like a fish hook. In his frantic twisting, he'd torn the flesh of the lid, and blood spattered my hands and his snout.

Tommy, who was always easily excitable, cried, "Oh God! He's going to lose his eye."

I held the dog's muzzle with my left hand and tried to work the wire free with my right, but the length and the stiffness of the wire made it too difficult, and I could see that I was only hurting him and making it worse. "Are we going to have to shoot him?" Tommy half whispered. "To put him out of his misery?"

It was what we'd always been told, of course, that if you couldn't stop an animal from suffering, you put him out of his misery with a bullet behind the ear. We'd all known ranchers who'd shot horses with broken legs. In fact, the idea held a captivating fascination for us that made us wonder whether we'd be brave enough to shoot an animal like the men around us had done. I could hear in Tommy's voice the slight desire to do the job. It didn't surprise me. I'd felt it myself.

The previous summer I'd come across a mare on the open range that had been struck in the neck by a rattler. She was standing along a fence, wheezing and drooling, her head hanging down, her neck swollen twice it normal size. I stood there with my .22 cradled loosely in my arm, but I was too young to complete the merciful act myself, so ran for help. The rancher who owned the horse was a man named Rutterman. We got in his pickup and I directed him to the horse. Rutterman didn't hesitate to take a revolver from the glove box of his truck and put the poor animal out of her misery.

I didn't think we'd have to shoot Lucky unless we couldn't find a way to get the wire out of his eyelid. I think I could have cut it out, but neither of us had a knife.

"Is Clive home?" I asked Tommy.

"I think so."

"Run and get him. Tell him what's happened. He'll know what to do. Hurry up! I'll hold the dog."

So, Tommy ran, and I watched him climb and disappear over one hill after another until he was out of sight completely. I sat holding Lucky, comforting him with my voice, keeping the tension off the wire to prevent more damage.

I was aware that I automatically thought of Clive rather than of Asa, whom I trusted more than anybody. I knew that

Asa was at work, however, and even though he would have left the PO and come to our rescue, it was natural to think of Clive first. As I said, he'd become the rescuer of kids, and I felt perfectly comfortable putting Lucky in his hands.

I don't know how long we sat there with the sun beating down on us. It seemed like forever, but Lucky sensed that I could help him, and even though he jerked his head from time to time, he remained mostly calm, and I talked to him the way I'd been taught to talk to an animal in stress, stroking his coat and letting my voice soothe him as cowboys do cattle by singing to them.

Clive's Dodge pickup bounced into view finally, and he had the sense to park along the dirt road twenty-five yards away and walk in, so as not to startle the dog. His size and bearing comforted me, and he smiled down on us from under a sweat-stained, wide-brimmed, white cowboy hat that he wore on the back of his head.

"What the hell have you boys gotten yourselves into now?"

"Lucky ran a wire through his eye lid. It's a long coil, and I don't know what to do."

"Here," he said, kneeling down. "Hold his mouth closed."

I held Lucky's mouth shut while Clive simply clipped the wire to about a three-inch length. He used the same wire cutters he'd used to cut the barbed-wire fence the day we poached those antelope. Taking hold of the end of the wire, with one quick motion, he twisted the wire from Lucky's eyelid, and let the dog run free.

"The bleedin's not serious," Clive reassured me, standing and sliding the wire cutters back into his jeans pocket.

"But have Asa wash the wound in alcohol tonight so's it don't get infected. That's the dog was thrown out of the car, right?"

"Right!" I answered.

"Well, he's a lucky dog, all right. I don't know if that means good luck or bad, but he's aptly named, I'll say that. I got to get on now. You boys stay out of trouble if you can." It seemed strange advice coming from a man whose middle name was trouble, but I thanked him as he strode away.

"Sure enough!" he said, and waved his hand in the air without looking back.

That night while Asa was bathing Lucky's wound, I asked him how a man could be so bad, fighting and poaching, but be so good to kids.

"Well, a man's a complex thing. He's made to hear three voices in his life: God's voice, Satan's voice, and his own voice. If he listens closely to God's voice, he'll have trouble, but it won't be self-imposed, and God'll help him work through it. If he listens to Satan's voice, he'll be mean and cruel, and he'll end up dead or in prison. If he listens to his own voice, he'll make a lot of mistakes, causing grief for himself and the ones he loves."

"Clive Svareland listens to his own voice more than he listens to God's voice. He ain't mean, but he's foolish, and he doesn't learn from his mistakes, so keeps on making the same ones."

"But," I protested. "Nobody can listen to God's voice all of the time. You told me yourself that we gotta trust our own judgment sometimes."

"That's right."

"Then we're all in for some grief."

"Yes," Asa nodded sagely. "We surely are."

The remainder of June passed quietly, with me spending much of the time alone, wandering through the hills around Powder River. I explored abandoned cabins, ranch houses and dilapidated barns, which were abundant.

A place that fascinated me was the empty ranch house of Rutterman, the man whose horse was bitten by the rattlesnake, and to whom I'd run for help. Shortly after shooting that horse, Rutterman raped his fifteen-year-old daughter, Louella, and got her pregnant. He went to prison. Louella moved away to have her baby, and we never heard of any of them again. We always wondered if she had an idiot child.

So Rutterman's place stayed vacant for about a year. I don't know why it took so long for somebody to buy it up, as it seemed pretty good land for running cattle. Maybe the water was bad out there, as it is in much of Central Wyoming. Maybe the fact that there wasn't a tree on the place and only bunch grass in the yard made it undesirable for a rancher's wife. Or maybe it was because nobody wanted to live in a house where a man had raped his daughter.

I spent a good part of one day out there. In one of the outbuildings I found some coyote and bear traps, rusted out, but still usable. I fooled with them, as traps are fascinating things, especially for a boy with time on his hands and a recently acquired what-the-hell attitude. Asa had warned me never to mess with traps, as the danger is great. We knew people who'd gotten their hands or feet caught in them, and if they didn't lose fingers or toes, and some did, their recovery was long and painful, and often they didn't get full use of their fingers back.

But that morning I stood in the dust of the outbuilding studying them, their teeth looking like the bared teeth of the very animals they were designed to trap. I held one side of a trap down with my foot, then pried the other jaw open with both hands until I heard the center pad click into place. The next moment was always the most frightening and exhilarating. I had to let go. I'd hold my breath, tense myself, and then leap back, spreading my hands up and away, half expecting to feel the cold steel close on my hands or feet. Mostly they stayed open, and I stood there listening to the wind bang a shutter in the barn and waiting for the dust to settle around the trap before I would spring it. But a number of times they didn't catch, and the teeth snapped angrily, missing my foot or my fingers by inches, the impact bouncing the trap up from the floor, the chain rattling like what I thought must be a death rattle.

When they did hold, I'd take an old broom handle or a two-by-four and press it down on the pad, triggering the mechanism, the teeth snapping on the two-by-four, holding it fast, or cutting the broom handle in two.

I'd heard about coyotes and rabbits that chewed their feet off to get out of a trap, only to die later anyway. I knew what would happen if I got caught in the trap, alone out there at Rutterman's without anyone to help; but I played with them anyway, deliberately flirting with danger, tempting fate, fascinated with the power of the springs. Throughout that summer I had a fatalistic outlook, believing that with my mother gone from our home, life wasn't much worth living.

After a bit I tired of my games and went into Rutterman's house where I ate my pocketed lunch in Rutterman's kitchen where an old wood table and one chair still stood, dust covered and forlorn. It seemed strange to know that not so very long ago a family had taken their meals right there where I was sitting. It seemed unnatural that all the living Rutterman and his family had done was blowing away with the sand, and that whatever warmth they'd experienced at Christmas or Thanksgiving or on someone's birthday was blowing through the broken windows by the relentless Wyoming wind.

I remembered Louella Rutterman and her sister, Doreen, as big, German girls who laughed easily and constantly pulled at one another's braids. I never got to know them very well, but they had seemed happy.

We never heard of any trouble in their family before the rape. But then nobody heard of trouble in my family either until the day my mother left. After finishing my sandwich, I walked into what was clearly a girl's bedroom. The bed frame and the spring still stood in one corner of the room. Some faded photos of James Dean and Marilyn Monroe were still tacked to the wall above the bed, and a girl's black shoe lay under it. I wondered if here was where the rape had taken place.

It's difficult for a boy to think about the reality of rape. It's completely foreign to most boys and not easy to imagine even. I mean, I'd heard about it only in general terms, and in those days mostly in whispers. It always sounded like brutal act it is, and I didn't dwell on the brutal acts of life. I puzzled over how any man could rape a woman, or would want to force himself on a woman. It certainly wasn't sexually exciting; not for me anyway, and I never discussed it with other boys except during Rutterman's trial and then we were completely unforgiving. I have always been both saddened and outraged by it, and have felt bad that women have cause to fear men, have cause to avoid being friendly or make eye contact with strangers.

And that afternoon, standing there in what must have been Louella's bedroom, I wanted to apologize to her for her father's unforgivable act out of some sense of universal guilt just at being male. I wanted to be able to reassure her by saying, "Listen, Louella, we're not all like that, and I would never hurt you." I walked home that afternoon sobered, and I never again returned to Rutterman's place, even though the lure of the traps called to me.

In October of that year a family named Armitage bought the place, tore down the old house and replaced it with a modern, double-wide mobile home. They ran cattle, and it made me feel good to see lights glowing on the site upon my late return from hunting.

Chapter Five

For a town of ninety-plus folks, Powder River was unusual in that it had four cultural centers which spoke to the various parts of our lives. The church, of course, met our spiritual needs. The American Legion Hall met the more primitive needs of sex, violence, music, wild laughter and dance. It covered more bases than even the church, to the great chagrin of Reverend Henderson.

The school obviously met our educational needs, but provided for some social needs as well. On Saturday nights when there was not a dance at the American Legion Hall, Herb and Rose Schmidt would invite the towns' people to watch movies. They were mostly educational films about science or wild life, or bare-naked men and women from Darkest Africa, or a narration on the teeming thousands in India. Once in a great while Herb would surprise us with an Abbott and Costello, or perhaps a western with Randolph Scott or Roy Rogers. Herb and Rose always popped fresh popcorn or provided a tub of chilled, crisp apples for everybody who attended.

But the real center of interest in Powder River in the 1950s was the Tumble Inn, a restaurant-bar-café rolled into one, owned by a man named Buzz Fister, who'd come west from Chicago where he'd made a bundle in the aluminum manufacturing industry, specializing in crutches and bicycle frames.

"Welcome to Powder River, A Mile Wide and an Inch Deep," the sign along the highway at the edge of town read. Underneath that was, "Home of the Tumble Inn."

The Tumble Inn was a log cabin with a short front step, which actually caused numbers of people to tumble in to the restaurant, especially drunk cowboys and pregnant women.

The inside of the building was cozy, with a low ceiling. It was warm in the winter and cool in the summer. The restaurant was in the center, the bar on the right, the café on the left. The log walls sported trophies of jackalope, antelope, deer and one moose; and one wall of the bar proudly bore the scrawled signature of world-famous bronc rider, Casey Tibbs, who won six national bronc riding titles between 1949 and 1955. His signature on the wall of the Tumble Inn was in itself a statewide attraction.

The Tumble Inn was also a financial and business center in central Wyoming at the time. Ranchers sold cattle and sheep to one another over a tabletop. Foremen hired hands at the bar. Trucks, horses and even whole ranches worth hundreds of thousands of dollars swapped hands, often with only a handshake to seal the deal. It was said that some days more money changed hands in the Tumble Inn than in the banks of Casper, and since it was the only restaurant in town, the Tumble Inn had something no one else had, waitresses.

Everybody recognized the fact that the waitresses at the Tumble Inn were not there only to serve food and drinks. They were there to tease, pinch and bed. Cowboys, truckers and linemen from the REA loved Tumble Inn waitresses. They were such a contrast to the solid, stable character of the ranch wife, whose life was often so hard as to rob her of her youth and beauty long before her time. So the waitresses were appealing, regardless of what they looked like. To most of the men, they were breasts, hips and legs under the standard brown and white waitress uniform. They had names like Katie and Babe, Mickey and Bunny. They came and went regularly, about an even half-dozen of them working for a year or two before moving on. It was, after all, a dead-end job.

"I never remember names of waitresses." Cowboys often joked. "Birthmarks, maybe."

Originally I tried to blame my trouble on the Tumble Inn, since Donna was a waitress there and that's how I met her. Then I blamed Asa, for he was the one who made me find a job; but looking back, I have to agree with Asa, who'd said it was because I stopped listening to the voice of God, and began listening to my own voice.

Donna Carlson was a waitress at the Tumble Inn for almost four years, a long time really. She was thirty-three the year I took up with her. She could not have children. Everybody knew that, of course. Not being able to have children was a major discussion topic among the women in the West.

Donna was married to Whitey Carlson, whose real name was Joe, but whose white hair gave him the nickname he lived and died with. He was a tough, wiry little guy with a reputation for the women, which everybody seemed to accept, even his wife, just as they accepted Clive Svareland's poaching. Whitey was just a woman poacher, is all. He worked a variety of jobs around Casper and Powder River, first driving for an oil tool company, then as a wildcatter on rigs in the area, and finally as a ranch gopher and handyman while he saved to buy his own place up in the Wind River Canyon near Thermopolis, where there were some pretty famous hot springs. It was Whitey I went to work for building fence and painting his barn, until I got in trouble with his wife.

I became aware of Donna when I was a freshman and began taking the bus into Natrona County High School in Casper. Some days upon my return home, I would stop in at the Tumble Inn and have a piece of apple pie in the café. The cook was from Germany, a man named Albrecht; a large, fat guy who'd eaten more than his share of the German pastries he'd baked all of his life.

So I'd go in there for pie and milk, and there were always cowboys sitting at the counter who would kid me the way men kid a boy who has grown up among them, jokes about getting to be handsome and a lady killer, and how the girls would have to watch out for me, and stuff like that.

Donna Carlson was my mother's friend for a while, but talk was that Donna was loose with the men, and my mother was pretty reserved about that kind of thing, so disapproved and kept her friendship on the distant side.

I had romantic and sexual notions about two grown women when I was in high school. Donna was one of them. The other was a teacher named Miss Jackson.

Miss Jackson wore her short, blond hair in a duck's tail. She was athletic, and physically appealing, with a great deal of energy and a smile that knocked my socks off. I used to pop into her classroom right after the last bell and we'd talk about my future and her past. She sat at her desk with me in a student desk facing her. She'd been quite a swimmer and tennis player when she was younger, and still could beat just about everybody in Casper. She won many local tournaments.

Talk was that she was queer, a lesbian, an almost unspoken term in those days along with abortion, rape and incest. Mostly kids talked about her being queer because she lived with another woman teacher, Miss Lawrence, who taught business classes. But it didn't matter to me if Miss Jackson was queer. I was crazy about her, mostly because she treated me so kindly, so adult. What she did, of course, was treat me like an individual, and when you're a kid and an adult treats you with respect, you appreciate it. So, for a while I thought I loved Miss Jackson, and knew in my heart that someday I'd make love to her so well that she'd quit being queer and would marry me.

Donna Carlson was the other woman I was crazy about. She was a small woman with long brown hair down to her waist, which she wore pulled back in a pony tail, or in one long braid to accentuate her butt. Donna was always packed into tight, blue jeans when she wasn't wearing her brown and white waitress uniform. She'd twitch her butt around the café, bringing comments from the men, comments I myself thought but never had the courage to speak aloud. She stood only five foot one and didn't weigh a hundred pounds. She was put together well in all the right places, and the men liked looking at her. Whitey didn't seem to mind either, as long as nobody touched her or made inappropriate comments within his hearing. I'd returned from walking the hills one afternoon in late June, and had stopped in for a piece of pie when she asked me if I was looking for summer work. Coincidentally, just a couple days before, Asa suggested I get a job. He didn't think I should just sit around and do nothing now that I was sixteen. Besides, since my mother left and took the Buick, I'd been after Asa to get me a car. He said that if I wanted a car of my own, I should be able to pay for half of it and carry the insurance myself.

Anyway, she just asked me if I was looking for work, and so I said yes and asked her what kind of work she had.

I was sitting at the café counter and she was standing across from me in her tight, little uniform, her breasts pushed up as she leaned on the counter before me. No one else was in the café at the time.

"Whitey wants someone to build a fence and paint the barn and the tack shed. Can you build a fence?"

"Sure!" I said enthusiastically through a mouthful of pie. "I build a good fence."

It was true too. I could work pretty well that way, building fences, sheds and helping with barns. I had a good eye for measuring, and I liked working with hand tools.

I was pleased on a number of counts that she would ask me. First of all, I really wanted to get that car. Secondly, I preferred building to working with stock. It's strange, but growing up in Powder River all those years, nobody ever asked me to work on a ranch. Nobody took interest to teach me about cattle and horses. Maybe it was clear to them that I never really liked the idea of ropin and ridin, although I always liked seeing it at rodeos and fairs. I think maybe I was intimidated by the size of the animals, and with their unpredictability. Maybe Hetty's accident had something to do with it. I don't know. I did, however, like western life, with the freedom and independence ranchers and cowboys always seemed to have. But no matter how much I appreciated and loved the West and its people, I never wanted to be a cowboy or do ranch work.

The third reason I was pleased was that Donna was talking to me alone without any of the men around. It was as if I was a man, and she treated me like she treated the rest of them.

"I've helped with lots of building hereabouts." I told her "You could ask around."

"Well," she smiled. "Whitey will be in here in a little while, if you want to wait. He's the one does the hiring."

"Okay, I'll wait," I said, pleased to have an excuse to be alone with her for a while longer.

"Good!" she answered, standing straight, stretching, pushing her breasts out for me to see. She arched her back, knowing exactly what she was doing, and even though I blushed, I looked at her boldly. For I knew what was going on, as a boy does even though he's never taken part. I'd seen the men tease and flirt with the Powder River women both in the Tumble Inn and at the Legion Hall, and I was more than willing to become one of them.

It's funny how we learn to be sexual. It comes natural, of course. You see your father and mother, other men and women, and at first it doesn't mean anything. Then you're embarrassed with it, and finally, in one way or another, you take part. Donna's stretching reminded me of a film I'd seen in a biology class, a film about female birds strutting and stretching, wiggling their tail feathers in preparation for mating. I recognized a mating dance when I saw one.

I called Asa at the PO and proudly told him I was waiting at the Tumble Inn for Whitey because I thought he might have work for me. Then I returned to my place at the counter and watched Donna sashay around the café, swinging her butt back and forth and moving around inside her waitress uniform in ways I thought remarkable.

It wasn't long before Whitey came in. He'd been hauling cattle for Sid Curry and had just come back from Casper. I never really liked Whitey much. I was always afraid of him. He was tight and dangerous, like the unsprung traps I'd played with at Rutterman's, and he always had a three-day growth of beard. You know how it is with blond men; it just makes their faces look dirty, not like they're growing a beard or anything. He always seemed ready to smash anyone who got in his way, and a lot of people steered clear of him.

"Whitey," I said in greeting as he walked in and plopped himself down on the stool next to mine.

"Howdy, kid. How are ya?"

"Fine," I answered nervously.

"Hey, Donna!" He called into the kitchen. "Come on out here and say hello. Your hubby's home."

Donna came out of the kitchen on the run, swept around the counter and threw herself into his arms, giving him a big, wet kiss. He'd stood up to take her onslaught and pulled her tightly to him, picking her up and swirling her around.

They did that a lot. They were always grabbing and kissing one another in public, always squeezing one another's butts and showing a lot of tongue with their kisses.

It was embarrassing mostly, but exciting too for a kid who hadn't ever French kissed in his life. For the boys at the high school, French kissing was a sign of something far more sexual than most of us ever imagined.

"Hi Honey." Donna said when they broke their kissing and came up for air. "How was your trip?"

"Slicker than pork fat through a goose," he said, kissing her neck hard. She pulled away. "Don't. You'll give me a hickey."

"Won't be the first time," he said, laughing.

She stepped away from him and said, "Whitey, Matthew here wants to ask you something. Let me pour you a cup of coffee, and I'll leave you two men to your business talk."

It made me beam to hear her say that, and I felt she respected me as the man I hoped to become rather than the boy I was. She poured the coffee and disappeared into the kitchen, leaving me alone with Whitey.

"So, what do you want, kid?"

"Well, Donna said you might need somebody to build a fence and do some painting, and I could really use the work. Asa said he'd help me buy a car if I worked this summer. I'm good at building, and I can paint a barn as good as anybody."

"I want a good job, kid, a really good job. I want to sell the land by summer's end, and haul that mobile home up to that place me and Donna are buying on the Big Horn River. So I want the place to look good. I don't want a half-assed job done by just any teenager."

"I can do the job the way you want it." I assured him, sounding less confident than I wanted to sound.

"Well, when can you start?" he asked. "I already got the lumber and the nails sittin in the barn."

"Tomorrow," I said. "I can start first thing in the morning."

"Can you be out there by six? I gotta be gone by seven, and I'll want to show you what I need done out there."

"I can be there."

"It's a deal, then," he said, and in the manner of men I'd known for years, he offered me his hand. I took it and shook hands, but he didn't let go when I thought we were done shaking.

"Aren't you forgetting something, kid?" he asked, keeping a firm grip on my hand.

Suddenly I was scared, afraid I'd botched the deal in some way. I'd clearly forgotten something important, and he knew it, being a man and used to dealing with other men.

"I don't know. What?"

"Well, you wanna get paid for your work, or are you doing it out of Christian duty?" And he laughed wickedly.

I was embarrassed, and felt such a fool I couldn't find my voice.

"I'll tell you what, kid. Rather than try to figure out that hourly crap, I'll give you a flat fee. I'll pay you $300. Whatta ya say to that?"

"That's great!" I said. "Three hundred is just great!"

"It's a deal then. You be there at six; and kid…"

"Yeah?"

"Don't ever take a job without knowing the pay. A boss'll respect you more if you ask him. Make it clear what you think you're worth. If it's too much, he'll let you know;

but more'n likely, you'll get what you ask for if you're fair. Understand?"

"I understand. Thanks. Thanks a lot, Whitey."

He finally released my hand which had begun to ache to the bones, and I ran all the way to the post office, more like a kid than a working man, excited to tell Asa about my job.

I had worked with men before, as I said, on barns and building fence; but I had never worked alone, in charge of my own planning and schedule. It made me feel older, part of the adult world. I talked all through dinner about it to Asa, recounting each detail, and every word that took place between me and Whitey. I was embarrassed to admit to Asa that I'd overlooked how much I'd be paid, but he waived it off.

"Hell, Matthew, we all had to learn it just like you."

I admit, however, that I never mentioned my moments alone with Donna or my thoughts about her.

That night I was too excited to sleep, and I thought a lot about becoming a man. It's something all boys get to merely by growing, but I knew too that the word meant more than just being a male adult. There were good men and bad men, strong ones and weak ones, wise men and foolish men. There was the opportunity to become a ladies' man, and there was even a breed called a man's man. It was all so unclear, and I was going to be a part of it. I believed I'd be a good man, not a man like Clive Svareland, but a man who would make Asa and Lydia proud I was their son.

I slept off and on, but much of the night passed with me thinking while watching the window for first signs of morning light, which would be my signal to rise out and pack my own lunch. And it wouldn't be just an apple and a piece of bread stuffed in my pocket; but a working man's lunch of sandwiches, fruit, potato chips, and coffee in a thermos.

Whitey and Donna lived about two miles north of us in a twelve-wide trailer house on fifteen acres of scrub land, good for browsing a few cattle, but not large enough to run what might constitute a herd.

I arrived ready for work about five forty-five, pulling in alongside their two vehicles, Whitey's Ford pickup, and their "54" Pontiac Chieftain. I could see the barn off to the west of the trailer on a flat piece of ground with stakes marking where the fence posts would be. Next to the barn sat a tack shed made over from an old, one-car garage.

It was a cool morning for late June the way mornings tend to be in Wyoming, with the wind blowing across the plains, rolling tumbleweed over the bunch grass and through the grease wood until it collects in the bottom strands of a barbed wire fence or up against a snow fence. I enjoyed the moment, sitting alone in Asa's truck singing along with the radio while waiting to start my first real job.

While I sat, I had a vague awareness of what it would be like to be there all day alone with Donna. I hadn't formulated any specific thoughts, but was aware of it and excitement rolled around in my belly.

Startling me out of my reverie, the door of the trailer opened and Whitey stepped out wearing only a pair of jeans.

"What some coffee?" he called to me. I nodded.

"Well, come on in then," he said, waving me in. I turned off the ignition and climbed out of the cab, following him into the trailer house. "Sit down," he ordered, pointing to a kitchen chair. "Coffee'll be ready in a minute."

He was finishing packing a lunch box, and for some reason it embarrassed me to see him shirtless and shoeless. That was strange, because I'd worked with shirtless men most of my life. It seemed the most natural thing in the world to do; but here in his kitchen with Donna somewhere in the trailer made me uncomfortable. Was she shirtless too? I mean they'd been in bed recently, hadn't they? Maybe they were actually doing it as I drove up and sat just feet away singing Blueberry Hill.

Whitey finished packing his lunch in a black, metal lunch box, making me keenly aware that I was only carrying a brown bag lunch.

"Did you bring a lunch, or are you going to run home?" he asked, turning from the counter.

"I packed one."

"Good thinking. It's good for a man to pack his own lunch. Never disappointed that way."

He disappeared down the hall toward the bedroom. The trailer was somewhat of a mess, with cowboy boots and white socks strewn across the living room carpet. Three empty Coors beer cans lay on their sides next to a green, vinyl easy chair, the stuffing of which showed at the ends of the arms. The place smelled heavily of cigarette smoke, stale beer and the coffee brewing in the electric percolator on the kitchen counter.

I sat alone at the kitchen table, which had a Formica top and chrome legs. The tabletop had cigarette burns all over it. The light was on over the stainless-steel sink, which was filled with dirty dishes. There was a small, dry cactus plant on the window sill above the sink.

I could see down the hall to the bedroom door. The door was closed, though not pulled tight. I could hear Whitey's voice muttering, and I could hear Donna's replies, soft and muffled, as if she were still in bed under the covers. I wondered if she and Whitey slept nude. I was still sleeping in white, jockey shorts in summer and pajamas during the winter. Whitey came out in a few minutes, his hair combed wet, but his face still unshaven. He was tucking a blue-plaid, western shirt into his belt-less jeans, and he had on a pair of heavy work boots.

He took two white mugs from a cupboard shelf and poured coffee for the two of us.

"How do you like your coffee?" he asked.

"Black with sugar," I lied, unwilling to admit that I took milk as well. "Sugar?" he asked mockingly. "What's the matter kid, aren't you sweet enough yet?"

He handed me my mug and pushed a sugar bowl toward me, then opened a drawer and removed a spoon. He flipped the spoon onto the counter near the sugar bowl and sat down across from me.

"Thanks," I offered.

"You had breakfast?" he asked.

"Yeah. Hashbrowns, eggs and toast," I boasted, proud of what I was sure a good working man's breakfast.

"I'll eat at the Husky Super Stop outside Casper. Do you know the Husky?"

"Oh sure. Asa and I eat there sometimes."

"Great place to eat," he said. "Good food, good prices. You can always rely on truck stops kid. Remember that."

"Thanks, I will."

Changing the subject he said, "I always liked Asa."

"Yeah, me too," I answered, and he laughed. "That's probably a good thing seeing's as you got to live with him."

At that moment Donna came walking down the hall, her long, dark hair hanging loose and wearing only a man's white western shirt. She was bare-legged and bare-footed, and I noticed her toenails were painted bright red. I was a little embarrassed at the intimacy of it, but excited too to see her like that. I'd never seen any woman's bare feet except for my mother's, and Lydia had never painted her toe nails or her finger nails. Despite the fact that Donna wasn't wearing any makeup, she still looked pretty to me, and I tried not to be obvious in my appraisal.

"Good morning, Matthew," she said, reaching into the cupboard for her own coffee cup.

"Good morning."

"Ready for work?"

"Yes ma'am," I answered, embarrassed further by the fact that I'd never called her ma'am before.

"What shift you got?" Whitey asked her.

"Eight to five," she answered, padding across the floor to pick up a pack of Lucky Strikes and a book of matches from an end table in the living room. She returned and sat down at the table, lighting up her cigarette. She took a drag and blew smoke out of one side of her mouth. I thought it looked cool.

I never knew she smoked, for I had never seen her smoking at the Tumble Inn. I was disappointed, for I had been taught that only women of low character smoked, although a few ranch women smoked and Asa didn't seem to think they had low character. Still, it was fascinating to watch her.

"What you haulin?" she asked Whitey.

"I'm gonna take some heifers to Glenrock and Douglas, then swing over to Lusk and pick up a bull for Sid."

"That's a full day's work," she said, blowing more smoke, this time in Whitey's direction.

"You ever smoke, Matthew?" she asked.

"No."

"Whitey neither."

"I don't know how you can stand those things," Whitey said, disgusted. "Coffin nails. You'll be dead before you know it. You ought to quit. It's a dirty habit, and expensive. You realize how much money you'd have if you put that money in a bank?"

"About as much as you'd have if you put your beer money there," she snapped back.

"Besides," she smiled, "you told me you like the taste of it when you kiss me."

He stood up and poured himself more coffee.

"Come on, Matthew. I'll show you where things are. We'll leave Honey here to her cigarettes."

I stood up, and Donna did too. As he passed her, he slapped her hard on the butt, grabbing a handful of cheek, and I saw that she was wearing black panties.

"Ow! Don't!" She complained. "You're mean. Besides, you'll embarrass the boy."

I hated it that she referred to me as a boy.

"You're not embarrassed, are you Matt? Matt knows a bare ass when he sees one," he said, laughing a nasty laugh.

"It's not bare," she protested playfully, and she slapped at him.

I blushed and headed for the door, making both of them laugh in that adult way I had not yet acquired. Whitey was right behind me.

"The barn's old, but a good one," he said as we approached it.

"A corral will make this place more sellable. It's gonna run a hundred and forty feet out, then three hundred feet over, then back to the barn. Be just right for a little ropin."

He pulled the big, double door of the barn open with one hand while holding his coffee cup in the other.

"The tools and lumber are here."

Neatly stacked in the middle of the barn were the posts and rails for the corral, two kegs of nails, several shovels, and a post hole digger. The barn was better kept than the mobile home, with harnesses and tack hung neatly on pegs, and tools standing in racks along the walls.

"You sure you can do this?" he asked me, sipping his coffee.

"Sure," I said. "I worked on Hyatt's fence, and helped Mr. Place with his."

"Okay, kid. Do a good job. Keep it straight."

Then he left me alone looking at the lumber and thinking it was a lot of fence. I walked around the barn, replaying in my mind the behavior I'd observed in the kitchen. Asa and Lydia kissed, not quickly either, but long, nice kisses. However, I'd never seen Asa grab my mother's butt.

I knew in some instinctual way that Asa and Lydia made love in their bedroom, but did they act sexy like Whitey and Donna when I wasn't home? I couldn't picture them doing it. It's not the kind of thing a boy can picture, his folks having sex, especially if the boy has never done it himself. I knew the excitement of close dancing, of hoping to feel girls up, of becoming hard in my blue jeans. I had the intimate moments with Betty on prom night, feeling her small breasts against my chest, feeling her close beside me. I knew well the excitement of imagining having sex, but didn't know any more than that, didn't know beyond an occasional magazine photo what a woman's breasts looked like really.

I thought about Donna and Whitey naked in bed together, remembered her in the white, western shirt, her legs bare and her feet soft and exciting looking. Thinking of her there in the kitchen, I wondered what it might be like to kiss a woman who'd been smoking.

Standing alone in the spacious barn, knowing that Whitey had gone to work, and thinking about what having sex must be like, I got pretty excited. I imagined myself with Donna over the next couple of weeks, imagined taking breaks from my work to share her bed and her body. She would teach me everything I needed to know to be a man with a woman, and we would declare our love for one another in actions as well as in words.

I knew in my heart it was just a boy's fantasy, knew a grown and experienced woman wouldn't have anything to do with me. So I resigned myself to my work and began hauling fence posts and rails out of the open barn doors.

I'd been digging post holes for about an hour when Donna stepped out of the trailer house wearing her brown and white waitress's uniform, waved to me, and drove off. I waved back and smiled at her, disappointed that she hadn't come out to me in her white western shirt and bare legs to offer me another cup of coffee.

I worked the day alone, proud that I was doing a man's job, and proud that I was responsible for all of it, and that when it was complete, I could take sole credit for the work. I knew that the men of Powder River would soon count me as an equal among them as they did Waxey Brown, who was only three years older than I. He grew up in Powder River, and like so many of the boys, stayed on to ranch with their fathers. Now Waxey drank with them in the bar of the Tumble Inn. It's what I had to look forward to I guessed.

Throughout the day my thoughts moved back and forth between what it meant to be a man among men, and what it would mean to be a man among women. I fantasized a lot about making love to Donna, or some yet unknown woman who would love me and let me love her and take care of her. I knew that somewhere between Asa and Whitey was the man I would become. I wouldn't grow dull and passive, as I suspected Asa had become for my mother, but neither would I be crude, like Whitey, though I wanted to be exciting to my wife as he apparently was to Donna.

Thus did my first full day working as a man, pass. At the end of it I was tired, but proud, and I looked forward with new confidence to the coming days, seeing the fence actually take shape, and knowing that I would have frequent contact with Donna.

Chapter Six

My work went well after I settled into a daily routine and made myself keep my mind on my task. I dug fence postholes for five sections of fence at a time, and then set the posts. We didn't use concrete mix, and I don't remember any rancher using it to fence off his land; but the posts had been dipped in creosote to help preserve them against the weather and insects. One thing I never understood about setting fence posts was that I never had any dirt left over. It didn't make sense to me, as the post should have displaced a certain amount of dirt; yet, when I had each post set with the dirt tamped down around it, there was no excess, not even a little mound around the base of the post. I asked Asa about it, and he spun a story about the Spirit of the Plains that exacted the price of a few shovels of dirt as payment for us dividing up the prairie unnaturally. Asa was a great, straight-faced liar when he wanted to be.

When I finished the first hundred and forty feet, Whitey slapped me on the back and complimented me on my work. The fence was true and straight, straighter he said than he could have done himself. It made me proud, as it was a compliment from a man other than my father in recognition of a good job.

By the end of the first week, my hands were beginning to get over the soreness and the blisters I'd acquired the first couple of days. My muscles too were growing accustomed to the work, and I was acquiring a good tan. I also thought I noticed more muscle definition in my chest, shoulders and arms. I worked mostly with my shirt off, as the afternoons were growing hotter, with the temperature rising into the low nineties, and forecasts calling for high nineties within the week.

Mostly I was alone. Whitey often hauled livestock from one ranch to another, along with tools and tack. Donna worked day shifts much of the time, but there were mornings when she didn't go to work until noon. Other days she worked the early morning shift and returned home about one, only to return to the Tumble Inn for the evening shift.

I was always aware when she was home, although for the first little while she never came out to speak to me. From time to time I would look up at the trailer house and she would be standing at the kitchen window watching me. She would wave, and I was excited just to return it.

Even though they'd told me I could use their bathroom whenever I needed it, I was afraid to approach the trailer when she was there, so went around behind the barn to urinate. When she was gone, I felt comfortable enough to use their toilet and get cold water at the sink, but never when she was home.

One afternoon I had gone in to refill my gallon water bottle and use the bathroom; and afterwards decided to look into their bedroom. I left the sink and walked down the corridor until I stood in the doorway, observing the unmade bed. The white sheet and a red blanket were entwined like contrasting human bodies. I moved closer to the bed, breathing quietly, sniffing the air for some human sexual smell, and listening for I didn't know what; lingering sounds of passion maybe, any remnant of what might have happened there before my arrival.

I noticed the bureau drawers half-opened, and focusing on them saw silky, colorful garments in one drawer, so after looking behind me and out the trailer window to guarantee my need to be alone, I opened the drawer further and examined the undergarments. I ran my hands through the panties and bras, excited at the taboo I was breaking. I picked up a pair of red panties, put them to my face and breathed through them, not knowing what to expect, and smelling only the odor of freshly laundered clothes. Sexual excitement and guilt swept over me at the same time, and I retreated to the sink for my water jug, returning to my work on the barn with the feeling that when Asa looked at my face that evening, he would know I'd done a bad thing.

Finally the fence was complete. Whitey was happy with it and even stopped off at the PO to tell Asa that I had done "a hell of a good job," and he praised me in the bar at the Tumble Inn to other men.

I was in the process of painting the barn when I began to notice that Donna was home more both mornings and afternoons than she had been while I'd worked on the fence. I guessed that she was working the evening shift a lot more often, and I was excited that she began to pay me more attention.

I would be painting without my shirt in the heat of the afternoon sun, and she would bring me out a pitcher of lemonade or ice water. She wore cutoff shorts, so short I could see her cheeks in two puffy crescents where her shorts ended. She wore sleeveless western blouses tied at the front and open in the throat, and she would stand below me while I was up on the scaffolding I'd built, and she'd chatter about nothing important, showing me a lot of cleavage and in general making me miserable.

One morning I'd arrived particularly early to paint four or five hours before the sun got to its hottest, the afternoons at that point being almost unbearable at a hundred and one degrees. I arrived at four when it was barely light, and parked next to the Pontiac, aware that the truck was already gone.

I stood in the semi-darkness looking at the mobile home, knowing she was alone inside. I had the sense that she was looking out at me too, but that was probably just hopeful thinking. A guilty conscience asked, *What are you gonna do, stand there all day?* Feeling foolish I got myself together and began to haul paint and brushes up to the scaffolding to start working in the cool, predawn light.

I'd painted for about an hour and a half when Donna opened the door and called to me from the trailer.

"Matthew?" her voice rang out across the prairie. I turned from my work to look at her.

"How long have you been up there?"

She stood framed in the doorway with one hand holding the door open. She was dressed in a blue and white plaid western shirt, but no jeans or shoes.

"Since about four," I answered.

"Did you have breakfast?" she asked.

"Yeah, I did."

"Do you want a cup of coffee?"

"Sure."

"Well, it's ready," she said. "Come on in and take a break."

I put the lid on the paint bucket and wrapped the brush in a damp rag to keep it moist, then climbed down and walked to the trailer. I found myself excited at the possibilities. My hands were shaking, and I was afraid my voice would betray me. I stepped inside, pulling the kitchen door closed behind me. She was seated at the kitchen table, smoking just as she had been my first day on the job.

"Good morning again," she said, smiling, holding her cigarette between two fingers in what I thought was a very sophisticated way. Her hair was brushed nicely and she was wearing fresh lipstick. It left a red print on the tip of her cigarette.

"Good morning," I answered.

"Sit down. I poured your coffee. You can put sugar in it. I remembered that's how you take it."

I slid out a chair and sat across from her. I picked up a spoon and spooned some sugar into my cup, hoping she wouldn't notice my hands shaking.

"Is something wrong?" she asked.

"Milk. Would you have some milk for the coffee?"

"Milk? Why sure," she said, rising from her chair and placing her cigarette on the edge of the table; and I could see how the table top had acquired so many burn marks.

"I'll get it for you," she continued as she opened the refrigerator. "I don't remember you using milk that morning you, me and Whitey had coffee together."

"I didn't ask for it. You know how the men at the café tease me about stuff. I was afraid Whitey would give me a hard time about it."

"I know exactly how you feel. I've certainly worked around enough men in my life. They're all constant teases," she said, laughing.

She stood, her back to me, facing the open refrigerator with her right hand on the top of the door, the light inside the refrigerator shining through her thin, sleeveless shirt, outlining the shape of her body. The rise of her legs, the sweep of her hip and the narrowness of her waist were all visible to me. Her bare legs and feet excited me, and I was ultra-aware that her toes were highlighted by bright red nail polish. She remained at the refrigerator with her back to me, both of us silent now, the motor of the refrigerator the only sound. She let me get my fill, then closed the refrigerator door and turned to me with the milk carton in her hand.

"Here you go," she said, stepping to me and handing me the quart carton.

"Thank you," I half whispered, my voice lost in the dryness of my throat. I sat there with the carton in my hand looking up at her, aware suddenly that in addition to fresh lipstick, she was also wearing face powder, and her eyelids were dusted with bluish-green mascara. I could smell her perfume, a faint, spicy odor unlike the sweet, syrupy scent so many of the high school girls wore.

"Put the carton on the table, Matthew," she said softly. I obeyed.

She reached out, palm up. "Give me your hand."

I put my hand in hers and she pulled me to my feet. I stood taller than she, but still felt so much the boy.

"Here," she said. "Put your hand here."

She turned slightly to slide my left hand inside the opened snaps of her shirt for me to cup her breast. It was hot under my hand, her nipple erect between my fingers.

"Feels good, doesn't it?" she whispered. "It does to me. Squeeze it harder, a little harder."

I squeezed her breast.

"Kiss me," she said. "Put your arms around me and kiss me."

Then we were kissing. Her mouth opened and her tongue darted between my teeth. I had both arms around her, my eyes closed, kissing her and tasting the foreign, but exciting blend of her cigarette smoke, coffee and lipstick. She clung to me, pressing against me, grinding into me. I slid my right hand down and felt her bare cheeks realizing for the first time that she wore no panties, and she made a sound in her throat.

I behaved instinctively, following her lead, surprised that despite my inexperience I seemed to know well enough what to do. She pulled away from me suddenly, and I thought she was going to object and somehow be outraged.

"I love you, Donna. I love you," I blurted out.

"I know you do, honey. Now come with me and show me just how much you love me. Come on."

She took my hand and lead me down the hall I'd ventured down alone just a week before. When we were at the side of her yet unmade bed, she faced me and unbuttoned my shirt, slipping it from my shoulders, letting it fall to the floor. She ran her hands over my chest.

"Such a man," she whispered, her lips against my shoulder. "Such a man."

She pushed me back on the bed and untied my work boots, removing them, then my socks, and finally pulled my jeans and my shorts from me. She fell on top of me, kissing my lips again, then moving to my neck, her long dark hair forming a tent over us.

And so I made love for the first time, believing I was in love, and believing I was loved. Finally I knew what all of the men and the women of the world knew before me, knew the secrets of the bed that until then I could only imagine.

But I knew too that I'd joined the ranks of the fallen, had become what Reverend Henderson had always referred to as Fallen Man. Until that moment the phrase had always been meaningless, an abstract phrase ministers used to keep people in line. Until then I had believed that Fallen Man was something I would never become. For me it always meant murder, rape, robbery, and deliberate, malicious violence against my fellow man, and I always knew I would never take part in any such behavior.

Whitey was gone for three days, and in those three days I learned all there is to learn about sex except the tenderness and caring that goes with it when two people really do love one another. In that time Donna never told me she loved me, though I told her repeatedly, for at the time, still young in life's complex experiences, I equated sex with love.

Love wasn't the only thing I misread. I was too young, excited and blind to put meaning to Donna's continued references to what other men liked. I was just proud she included me among the men of the world.

"All the men love this. They just love it," she'd say, then show me a new sexual position or act.

"You're like the rest," she'd whisper. "You just love it, don't you?"

She was right. I did love it, so didn't pay attention to the fuller meaning of her words. I focused only on the excitement of the moment.

I knew I was doing what all men before me had done. Just as I was doing a man's job on the fence and the barn, I was doing a man's job in bed. So, in the three days Whitey was gone, I did it all.

The evenings were long and difficult for me. I was anxious to get back to Donna; but more importantly, I had serious secrets from Asa, my mother, and the people in the church who'd always said what a fine boy I was, as people do when standing around in front of a church on Sundays when you're a kid.

Reverend Henderson chose that time to give yet another one of his sermons on adultery, and it seemed it was directed right at me. It made me feel that he and everybody in Powder River knew what I was doing. While I was in Donna's bed, I foolishly ignored what I knew of living in a small town, that the truth would be out sooner or later, and most likely, sooner. Asa thought I was sick with fever, thought I'd spent too many hours painting in the hot sun without my hat on, but he didn't press it. I told him I'd make sure to wear my hat and drink more water; and I went to work and returned each day as usual, making sure I was never late arriving home.

Besides, Whitey had come home, and upon his return I never again had any intimate contact with Donna, despite the fact that she was home much of the time and Whitey was gone all day. She would bring me lemonade or ice water, and stand and chatter about the weather or Whitey, or something meaningless, but she never once mentioned our trysts.

I didn't understand her change of attitude, and attributed it only to the fact that Whitey was home every evening, but even when he went on the road again the following week for two days, Donna went to work and stayed away from me.

I began to feel awful, as it came clear to me that I'd been used. Her words about other men took on their truthful, terrible meaning, and my mother's distance from Donna slowly made an ugly sense. Miserably I finished painting the barn, but never got to work on the tack shed.

Saturday morning, a week later, I paid a man's price for a man's sins. Asa was at the PO, and I was at home sitting in the side yard, reading. Lucky lay at my feet, when I heard Donna's voice screaming in terror, and looked up to see her running along the road toward me in her brown and white waitress uniform, running desperately and without dignity. As I watched her, I was embarrassed at her ungainliness.

I couldn't make out what she was saying. Short of breath as she was, only the first part of her sentence carried to me. I dropped my book, jumped up and ran through the house and out the front door to meet her.

"Run!" She gasped. "He knows! He knows!"

She had her right hand on my shoulder for support, and she kept gasping for air. Initially I thought she meant Asa, that Asa had learned of our behavior, and I couldn't understand why I'd run from Asa. Then I saw Whitey's pickup throwing dirt as he sped up the road toward us.

I didn't run, of course. Where would I have gone? Besides, in my youth I believed that I needed to protect Donna, that she was the one he was going to harm, so I stood there stupidly as Whitey slammed the truck to a sliding stop.

As he leapt out of the truck, leaving the driver side door wide open, I stepped in front of her heroically and started to say something brave and noble when he lowered his head and dove into me, knocking me flat and landing on top of me, driving the breath out of me. He jumped up immediately and waited, his fists in leather work gloves bunched before him.

"Get up you little son of a bitch! You get up. I'm gonna beat the living shit out of you. You want to play a man's game, you take what's comin like a man. Get up."

Donna tried to step in front of him. "No, Whitey! He's only a boy."

He pushed her face with his open hand, sending her sprawling on her back, her legs shooting up, and one of her uniform shoes flew off her foot.

Struggling to get my breath, I got to my feet and raised my fists, knowing I couldn't do anything against him, knowing I wouldn't even try. He was right. I'd committed adultery, coveted another man's wife, and now I was going to get my just reward.

It's amazing what thoughts can go through your head at such a moment, and I thought of David in the Bible, and his time with Bathsheba, and then my thoughts shifted and I figured Reverend Henderson would be proud of me for taking my punishment willingly.

Then Whitey hit me a straight left hand and broke my nose. I didn't go down. His punch, solid, swift and true, blinded me and drove me backward, and though I couldn't see anything through the tears, I continued to face him. I'd never known such pain. It felt as if he'd driven my nose far into my head. I couldn't breathe, and I was swallowing blood. He followed up with a left-right combination, splitting both my eyebrow and my lips, spinning me away from him. I don't know how I stayed on my feet, but deep inside I knew why. I was convinced that I had it coming, was convinced I had to take the punishment I had earned. A good man would have done so, and although I had become a bad one, it meant something in the way of atonement for me to stay on my feet.

I could hear Donna crying, could hear other voices, men's voices, but I couldn't see anything through the red film that had washed over my eyes, which were now swelling shut. I wasn't even sure I was facing Whitey anymore.

I had seen a bull slaughtered a couple of years before, and to bring him down the rancher had hit him a startling blow in the head with a sledge hammer. The bull staggered about six and eight steps crookedly before falling, but I didn't fall. Being the experienced fighter he was, Whitey knew what he was doing. He hit me in the chest, on the arms, in my ribs; hurting me terribly, but keeping me on my feet for as long as he could. Finally he hit me once more in the face, and mercifully, I collapsed. Everything was spinning. Bright lights and stars flashed red behind my eyelids.

Sounds ran together: curses, cries, sobs, and scuffling sounds. Somebody was crying out, "I'm sorry! I'm sorry.

Oh, my God, I'm so sorry." I realized it was my own voice pleading through the blood and the dirt in my mouth.

It was Mr. Place, Hetty's dad, who saved me. Whitey, in his blind fury, would have beaten me to death. He just didn't know when to quit. Mr. Place pulled him off me, and when Whitey tried to continue, Mr. Place picked him up bodily and slammed into the back wall of Hyatt's store, holding him up off the ground. Outweighing Whitey by over a hundred pounds made it easy for him, although lots of fat guys wouldn't have had the power, but Mr. Place was deceptively strong, and he was madder than hell too, seeing Whitey work me over like that. He told Whitey that if he didn't let up, he'd kill him; and apparently Whitey believed him, because according to Hetty, Whitey just slid down the wall of the store to the ground and sat passively. I think the fight was out of him by that time, his arms being weary and all.

They loaded me into Mr. Place's Cadillac and picked up Asa at the Post Office to drive me to the hospital in Casper. It was the first time since Asa took the job in 1946 that he closed the PO early on a Saturday morning.

At the Natrona County Hospital they stitched my eyebrow and taped my lip, worked on my nose, and discovered that I had broken ribs, so taped them as well. They checked me over in general, cleaned me up and sent me home with some pain killers to get me through the first days of my recovery. Asa and Mr. Place didn't take me home, but instead drove out to Place's ranch, as they were reluctant to leave me alone in our house while Asa was at work, afraid Whitey might get it in his mind to return and wreak more havoc, although there was little chance of that.

He'd spent his fury. Besides, within two weeks, Whitey and Donna moved up to that place on the Wind River Canyon, the place he'd been putting payments on in recent years.

It ended up that I spent the rest of the summer out there at Place's, first convalescing, then working as a handyman and being a companion to Hetty.

I was not, however, much of a companion for the first little while. I stayed in bed for three days, too beat up and sore to move. Then I sat in the yard in the sun for another week. Mrs. Place insisted that I get a lot of sun and fresh air, said it would hurry the healing process. So for a while I didn't do anything except take little walks with Hetty, or sit in the sun listening to her chatter about what it was going to be like in our senior year, which I couldn't show much interest in at the time.

I tried not to think at all, really, tried to keep my mind blank or focused on the immediate, physical world around me. I counted fence posts in one direction as far as my eye could see, and then I'd turn carefully in my chair and count them in the opposite direction. I counted boards in the barn. I watched prairie dogs and gophers forage, and I studied birds in flight. I watched my shadow slowly cross the yard, lengthening and shortening as the day passed.

I didn't want to think about what I'd done, or the betrayer I'd become. I hated knowing that I'd let down the people who'd believed in me, and that hurt as much as my physical wounds; but mostly I knew I'd betrayed myself, and I would never again be able to feel as good about myself as I once had. I had become Reverend Henderson's Fallen Man, and I didn't know how I was going to get up.

For a while I didn't think neither my body nor my spirit would ever heal. I had difficulty facing myself, and certainly didn't want to face others. I felt sorry for myself as well, and wallowed in self-pity until Asa and Lydia set me straight.

Asa came out to see me every night the first two weeks. When I was able, we took short walks together; and three weeks after my beating, Asa began the process of repairing my psyche.

We were walking out south of Place's barns down a dry riverbed. I was pretty much tormented by shame and hadn't spoken much. We were walking pretty slowly on account of me being so sore, the stiffness still holding rein on my movements. It was a dead, calm evening, hot with heat lightning making streaks in the sky over the Seminoe Mountains far to the south. I was waiting for Asa to talk, but he didn't, and in a need to break our silence, I told him how I felt.

"I feel awful, Asa. I hurt inside. I don't mean only my ribs and all, but here," I said, thumping my chest. "Here in my heart there's an ache I can't really describe. I've done so badly. I don't think I'll ever be able to look myself in the eye again. I haven't looked in a mirror since I been out here, not even when I wash my face in the morning. I don't ever want to see any of the folks in Powder River again. I don't want to go back to school in the fall either. Maybe we can move to Riverton or somewhere. I've been such a fool. What am I going to do?"

He didn't speak for a while, and we walked further along the riverbed, our eyes before us on the sandy ground, or watching the heat lightning in the mountains. In fact, I didn't think he was going to respond at all, that I was going to have to do more talking, when finally he told the one bad thing he'd done as a boy that almost ruined his life.

"I robbed a store when I was sixteen," he said suddenly. "Armed robbery. I used a .22 pistol."

I stopped walking and studied him from behind, as he'd continued walking a few steps ahead of me. Then he turned and waited for me, but I didn't move, so he kept on walking away from me, and I was forced to follow his lead.

"To this day I know it wasn't ever the right thing to do, but it seemed like a good idea at the time. We were living just outside of Lander over in Fremont County, me and my brothers and my mother. My father had run off by then, and as oldest I felt I should be providing for the family. It was in the heart of the Great Depression, 1934, and none of us was making enough to eat very well, so I got it into my head that I could rob a store and get us some money and get outta there. I didn't think at all really, and just like you, I was listening to my own voice, not the voice of God, and certainly not even to the voice of reason."

"So one evening I took this .22 we had and I walked up to the highway toward Lander and held up a man I'd known all my life, a man who'd been kind to us and given us groceries when we didn't have money. His name was Lance Pettit. He owned a general store just outside of town. I walked in there and said, 'Lance, I'm sorry to have to do this, but we just can't live like this any longer. Open the till and give me the money and I won't have to shoot you.'

"Lance punched the No Sale button on the register and stepped back. Never said a word. I took the day's receipts.

You know how much I got? Twelve dollars. It wasn't a lot of money. Not even then."

"I realized, of course, that I'd become a robber, a thief, and had to get out of there; so I headed on foot down to the rail yard to hop a freight. I never once even considered taking the money home to my mother first."

"Took me twenty minutes to get to the rail yard, and sure enough, the sheriff was sitting in an open boxcar dangling his feet just waiting for me to show up. Stupidest thing I ever done, before or since. It humiliated my mother and made me feel like the lowest creature alive. Pretty much the way you feel now, I expect."

I studied his face as he talked, his face was terribly serious, and his eyes sad as he told his story. I was amazed at the revelation, for I'd never heard it before, and I never in my life imagined Asa would do so bad a deed. It was clear to me, however, why he was telling me the story now. I'd been feeling like I was alone in my actions, feeling I was the only one to commit such a sin, and Asa was letting me know that even the best of us were susceptible to sin. He was letting me know that sin wasn't just some abstract quality out of the Bible, or out of one of Reverend Henderson's sermons, but that we were, all of us, fallen. More importantly, Asa was telling me that we could rise up and once again become good men and women.

"What happened?" I asked him.

"The sheriff, his name was Coats, put me in jail overnight. My mother came out to see me and cried until he sent her home. Next morning he drove me back to Pettit's General Store and made me apologize and give back the twelve dollars. Then he drove me out to a work farm where they sent bad boys in those days, and I spent the next three months irrigating, putting up hay, and doing general farm work. I was never officially charged, never went to court, have no record."

"At the end of the three months he drove out one afternoon and told me I could go home. My mother and family were going to move to Casper and wanted me to go with them. On the drive to my house he told me about the three voices I've always told you about: God's voice, Satan's voice, and your own voice. He's the one told me that if I listened too much to my own voice, I'd cause grief and suffering, and he was surely right. Sadly, we all have to learn the truth of that."

"You see, Matthew, you ain't the only man ever to mess up, to cause himself and others to suffer. We all done something, and we all have had to become adult enough to live with it. You gotta put it behind you. Eventually you gotta go back to the church, gotta walk into Hyatt's, gotta eat at the Tumble Inn."

"I can't, Asa. I can't do that. I don't ever want to face those folks again."

"I know you don't want to, but it's what you have to do if you're ever gonna get over this. Everybody in Powder River knows you ain't fully to blame for what happened. Everybody knows that Donna Carlson bears a great deal of the responsibility. We all know what kind of a woman she is. Even Whitey knows it. Now they're waitin to see what kind of a man you're going to be, and they're hopin you'll have the courage to return to Powder River and take up where you left off. You don't have to do it today or tomorrow, but you gotta do it; and the sooner the better. The longer you wait, the harder it'll be."

We turned back, and I began to think about what my father had told me.

"What about Lydia?" I asked. "What about her? You said we all have done something awful, something to cause grief, like me with Donna and you robbing the store. Mother never did anything like that, did she? What did she do?"

"She left us."

As we made our way back toward Place's ranch, I began to see that he was right, and that my recent behavior was due, in part at least, to her leaving in April. I can't honestly say that her action caused me to take up with Donna Carlson. That isn't the whole truth. The truth is that I was interested in doing what I did. I wanted to know all about sex, wanted to have what I knew all the men in the world had, and Donna Carlson made it available to me. I recalled the Bible verse about Cain killing his brother. "Sin is crouching at your door," God said. "Its desire is for you, but you must overcome it." My actions were, indeed my own fault, I couldn't deny it, and yet, my mother's rejection of me and Asa was a major contributing factor.

So I took some comfort in my father's words, took comfort in knowing that I was not alone a fallen man, but that we were all fallen, even those we love the most. It did continue to bother me, however, that Asa had done nothing terrible in reaction to Lydia's departure. He never went out and got drunk, never took up with another woman, instead he had remained steady, listening to God's voice in him rather than to his own. I wished I could have been more like him, and I vowed to try harder to walk in his footsteps in the future, regardless of what happened to me.

Although it was Asa who encouraged me to take the first step, it was with Lydia that I actually took it. A week after Asa and I talked I was sitting on Place's porch reading the Casper Sunday Tribune. Hetty and her family had just left for church and I had the house to myself. They hadn't been gone ten minutes when I noticed dust being raised by a vehicle coming back along the road, and I surmised that Hetty had forgotten something. I watched the dust cloud approach, and from it emerged our old Buick, the one Lydia took the day she left. I dropped the newspaper on the porch and stepped down to watch her draw near, wondering what I was going to say to her, and what she would say to me.

She pulled into the front yard, stopping just short of what passed for lawn, shut off her motor, and sat there looking at me without speaking. She was wearing a white dress and a white, broad-brimmed, straw hat with a fresh, yellow rose stuck in the hat band.

I walked toward the car, stopping a few feet away to look at her. She smiled a full smile. She was a beautiful woman, and I realized just how much I loved and missed her. Pain registered in her eyes when she saw the yellowing bruises of my face and the stitches still in my eyebrow and lower lip.

She pushed the door of the Buick open and stepped out. She took me in her arms and hugged me. I buried my face in her neck and sobbed, and she held me for what seemed like the longest time, saying nothing, just holding me tightly. When I was cried out, and finally stepped away from her, she said, "You sure do look the worse for wear."

"You should have seen me two weeks ago."

"I wanted to come immediately, but your father encouraged me to wait, and although I don't know if he was protecting you or me, I think he was right."

I nodded my understanding, and suddenly felt a wave of guilt wash over me. I looked away.

"Do you like my outfit?" she asked, twirling around so that her skirt flared out.

"It's new. I bought it especially for this occasion."

"You bought a new dress just to come out here to see me and my puffy face?"

"I bought it to come here to take you and your puffy face to the Powder River church. If we drive like mad, we'll still get there before Asa finishes playing the first hymn."

I looked at her for a minute.

"I'm not dressed for it," I offered as excuse.

"I don't care."

I smiled enough to feel the stitches in my lip pull. "I'm afraid to go." I confessed.

"Me too," she said. "I haven't seen any of them since spring. I know they haven't thought kindly of me."

She waited. I shifted my stance and looked out over the prairie where the cattle gazed, looking thoughtless in the morning sun. We said nothing for a moment or two.

"I can put on a white shirt while you drive," I told her.

"Hurry. We can drive into Casper afterwards. I'll buy you dinner at the hotel."

It was that simple. She did drive like mad, and we did get to the church before the opening hymn was finished. They were singing, "Beautiful Savior, King of Creation" when we walked down the center aisle and took our old seats behind Asa. The singing faltered just a bit, but the piano never did; in fact, the music surged as we stood behind Asa, and I realized that Asa had been expecting us, had in fact, been involved, that Lydia alone didn't make the decision to contribute to my rescue.

The service was difficult for me, and my throat had a considerable lump in it from time to time. Tears blurred my vision periodically as well. Once or twice I thought I wasn't going to be able to see it through, but both Asa and Lydia sensed it. He grabbed my hand one time, and she grabbed the other hand the next, and for one hour we were once again a family, Asa and Lydia Christman and their son, Matthew, late of Place's ranch, returned to Powder River, the prodigal come home. Sitting there between them my awareness grew that both Lydia and I were prodigals together.

Members of the congregation who had seen me grow up, greeted me evenly afterwards, not as warmly as earlier in my life, but sincerely just the same. Hetty and her folks were proud of me, I could see, and Hetty made me choke up when she hugged me and kissed my cheek in front of everybody.

Folks were decent to Lydia, though notably cooler than to me, and I sensed it wasn't only their disapproval of her leaving that caused their reaction, but her expensive dress and broad-brimmed hat as well, and there were a few who resented that she had the audacity to return at all. She just wasn't as humble and contrite as they thought she should be.

That afternoon, my mother and I had dinner at the Gladstone Hotel in Casper, where she'd been singing since spring. She introduced me to the waiters and other hotel people she'd come to know. I was proud to meet them, pleased to see that she'd made a place for herself and was willing to include me in it.

It's not to say that I was suddenly and miraculously healed because Asa and Lydia saw and met my need; but the healing began that Sunday, and although I still lived with a great deal of guilt, I sensed that eventually my life would get back to normal. I knew the process would be slow and long, and I knew as well that the emotional pain I lived with would last far longer than the physical pain Whitey had dealt me.

What I learned from my mother and my father late that summer was that the love and forgiveness of God was made manifest through the love and forgiveness of the people who cared for me. In addition, the people of Powder River continued the process that Asa and Lydia began, somewhat reluctantly in some quarters, but eventually they took me back into their community. It helped that I was beaten senseless, as it provided physical evidence that God had already punished me, and they certainly didn't want to add insult to my injuries.

The men were quicker and better about it than the women. Men understand and accept men's faults and stupidities better than women do, better than women do even of their own faults. The women of Powder River needed to punish me for a while longer. Though polite and sympathetic, the look in their eyes said, *You've become one of them now,* as if I'd joined an enemy camp, marched now in the ranks of the men who'd betrayed them since biblical times. They were proud that I'd fulfilled the prophecy handed down to them by their mothers and grandmothers before them, and which they were in turn handing down to their daughters that very moment. Men were not to be trusted. Though good, men were weak when it came to liquor and women. They couldn't help themselves. Ignore the fact that the person I'd slept with was first a woman, and secondly a married one who'd betrayed her husband. That, however, seemed a different matter altogether.

For you see, there were many kinds of women in the world, good women like themselves and bad women like Donna Carlson, the whores of the world. And of course, there was Lydia, who had abandoned her family. The women of Powder River belonged to the Alliance of Good Women, those long-suffering women whose role in life was to be the good wife and mother, *in sickness and in health, for richer or for poorer, in good times and in bad.* It was the role allotted them, and a role they took seriously. They couldn't understand a Donna Carlson any more than they could understand Lydia leaving her husband and son to sing at the Gladstone Hotel.

Even Rose Schmidt was suspect, for although the women of the town could respect her as a school teacher who helped their children in ways they themselves couldn't, she didn't have any children of her own. She didn't keep a home as such. She worked, just as Donna worked. So though she was respected, she was never included as a member in good standing of The Alliance.

With the men of Powder River it was different. Their eyes said, "Welcome to the club." The club was actually the auxiliary to the Alliance of Good Women. It was not, however, the Alliance of Good Men. It went beyond that.

The look I read in their eyes said, *Welcome to the Club of Life. Now you know the suffering and the pain, because you are responsible for some of it. Now you know the guilt. You are Adam and Jacob, David and Judas. Now you understand the need of Christ on the cross, and you'll be different from here on out.*

Though I was becoming one of them, I was not yet their equal. That would come later when I'd borne and survived even heavier burdens. And so throughout the month of August, whenever I entered the Tumble Inn or Hyatt's, the men greeted me warmly. Have a cup of coffee. Sit over here. How you comin' along?

The women, on the other hand said, Good morning, Matthew. *I see your face is healing. Give my regards to your father.*

By late August my stitch marks were fading, my nose had gone back to a semblance of its original shape, and my ribs hurt only when I picked up something or moved suddenly. I was becoming whole again. I knew I would look different, would carry the scars of July for as long as I lived. For just as my physical scars would become part of my outward appearance, I knew the internal scars would forever rub against the inner walls of my heart.

Chapter Seven

Hetty Place and I became dear friends that summer. We never again tried to recapture prom night, but became true brother and sister of the heart.

Hetty rode with me into Powder River and Casper on errands for her father. She walked with me over the prairie surrounding the ranch house. I learned more what it was like to be around a girl, and in later years after I was married, I knew the comfort I felt with my wife was attributable in part to the summer I spent with Hetty.

When I think of her now, I think of her as a spiritual, almost holy child, set apart not only because of her flat head, but because of an inner depth the rest of the girls I knew at Natrona County High School lacked. We moved around one another comfortably. When I arrived all beaten and ugly, she cried and was sympathetic to me. Later, as I recovered, she became more observant of me, studying me, asking me questions about boys.

"Do boys worry about how they look? Do guys at school like the sound of their voices? Does it scare you to know you're going to be a man and have to do man kinds of things?"

As the weeks passed the school year loomed on the horizon, and I began to see in Hetty a beauty I only used to hope she would eventually have. She continued to wear her hair permed out and wavy to soften the flatness of her head. She got new glasses; still thick, but with more attractive frames to enhance her eyes; and she began what she called her "make up plan." Her mother allowed a bit of rouge or face powder to add color and soften her scars, but when we were away from the ranch, Hetty applied a pink lipstick and some green eye shadow, and then removed every trace before returning home. She had filled out more too, and I thought she looked very much like the rest of the girls at the high school. They sensed it as well, and included her more as one of them during our senior year.

Only once in the summer did Hetty make reference to my episode with Donna Carlson. We'd gone in to pick up halters and bridles for her father. Hetty's make up plan was in full bloom, and she said, "There's no point in putting on my face unless I can show it off a little. Let's stop at Woolworth's for a soda." So we did, and we were sitting at the counter sipping raspberry sodas when she asked, "Matthew? May I ask you a question about what happened this summer?"

"Sure," I assured her, uncomfortable as hell.

"Did you love that woman?"

"No," I said, unable to look at her. "I thought so at the time, I suppose; but it wasn't ever love. I can see that now."

"Hmmm," she said. "Well."

And that was it. Neither of us ever spoke of it again.

In addition to driving and delivering for her father, Hetty and I also spent a number of afternoons helping Mrs.

Place put up tomatoes, green beans, pickles and two boxes of peaches brought from Washington State by a neighbor who had travelled to see her sister. It was an even, peaceful time for me, without the anxiety and tension the first part of the summer had held.

When we weren't working for her father or working with her mother, Hetty and I walked a lot. One afternoon in late August we were out looking for wildflowers for Hetty's dried flower arrangements. It was a thing she did well, and even after these many years I still have one she gave me that summer.

We were walking along a narrow, black-topped, secondary road and came upon a curve where the road dipped, crossed what had once been a river bed, and climbed up the other side. It was the kind of spot that can be difficult to handle in a loaded truck, which must have been the case for someone, because there were new boards scattered along the curve in the road. It amounted to quite a bit of lumber, and we suspected that whoever lost it would be back later to pick it up. A number of boards still lay on the road proper, and we thought it could cause a serious accident for somebody driving along the road too fast, which folks do a lot in rural areas. So we decided to push the boards further down off the roadside.

I was going to do it, but Hetty insisted on helping, even though she could lose her balance pretty easily. So we picked up the boards one at a time, one of us on each end, and flipped them down into the barrow pit. A number of them overlapped, and as we removed the top of a group of about six two-by-sixes, we were surprised to see a fat snake half-exposed under the remaining lumber. He'd crawled under to escape the heat, and we disturbed his siesta.

"A rattler," Hetty said, flipping the board out of my hands and sending it down with the others.

No sooner had we uncovered it than it pulled itself further under the shelter of the remaining boards, its warning rattling softly.

"We should kill it," I said. "Let's go back to the ranch and get a gun."

"But the guy who lost the lumber could come back for the wood and get bit."

"Right," I agreed. "Hell, I wish I'd brought that .22 pistol of your father's."

We stood away from the lumber, alternately looking at the lumber and then both ways along the road hoping for a rancher with a rifle in the gun rack of his pickup. I squatted down and peered from a distance into the shadows of the boards. I could see the snake move slowly into a coil, could see his yellow, green and gray markings. We continued to hear the faint whisper of his rattle. I stood up.

"Why don't you walk back and bring a rifle," I suggested. "I'll wait here in case the guy comes back."

"Oh Matthew, I don't want to walk back alone, and I don't want to leave you here either. What if you need me?"

Hetty had been taking care of me all summer and apparently had decided that I couldn't take care of myself. So I made the kind of decision a kid makes, the kind you wouldn't make later in life when common sense makes more sense. I walked down to where a few boards lay shattered, and picked up a split two by four with a sharp point. It was an eight-footer. I waved it back and forth in the air a few times to get the feel of it, and then handed it to Hetty.

"Hold this a minute," I said.

"What are you going to do?"

"We're going to kill the snake," I answered, stepping away from her and picking up another full two by four, which I used to uncover the rattler by pushing the boards that covered it away. It rattled louder in clear warning that it would strike, as it was designed so well by God to do.

"Stay back," I ordered Hetty, which was basically unnecessary, as she was already ten feet further down the road.

"Oh, Matthew! I think we should go back and get a gun after all."

"No, no! We can do this," I assured her, excited now with the foolish challenge I had set for myself.

"I saw a cowboy once who hypnotized a rattler by passing a stick back and forth in front of its eyes. It focused on the end of the stick and didn't see the cowboy at all, didn't see the hand that held the stick, but only the point of the stick. They have bad eyesight you know."

"Oh, Matthew!" Hetty whined again.

I took the split board from her and approached the rattler, which was tightly coiled now, its rattle chattering out its warning more insistently than earlier, and I began to swing the board back and forth in front of me as I approached the snake ever so slowly, and sure enough, the snake's head began to weave back and forth following the tip of the broken board. I advanced on the snake one half-step at a time, all the while keeping the board moving. The snake's head swayed, following the stick until I had the spear point of the board just six inches from the snake, whose head had drawn back to strike when I plunged the stick into its head and pinned it to the sand. I yelled at the same instant, releasing the tension I hadn't known had built up in me. Hetty screamed once while the snake writhed and coiled over itself, its head buried, its body twisting and curling more and more slowly as its life ran out.

I let the board drop, and it remained stuck in the ground. I walked back to Hetty. She hugged me hard, and I held her for a moment. We both were shaking, so we sat down on the road holding hands and waited for the snake to be still. Finally, its death throes became a series of twitches, and finally ended. I got up and pulled the board from the sand. The snake's head was literally gone, but the body stuck to the board point, so I held it up high in the air for Hetty to see.

"Oh, that's awful," she said, turning away.

I carried the snake further off the road and threw the board out onto the prairie, then climbed back up to the road, and we headed off toward the ranch.

"I should have cut off the rattle and kept it as a souvenir," I said, remembering the scissors Hetty had brought along for the wild flowers.

"I'm glad you didn't," Hetty said. "I don't think we should even tell Daddy. He'll be mad."

"You're right," I agreed. "Absolutely right."

I realized how foolish I'd been, and was a little ashamed to have taken such a risk; but it is the kind of thing we do in our youth, and only reflect on afterward.

At the moment I was still excited, still exhilarated by my experience. My arms felt weak, but I also had a fluttery sensation in my chest. As we walked back along the narrow country road, holding hands without speaking, I wondered when I would ever learn to have better judgment. I knew Hetty was right, Mr. Place would be furious if he learned what I'd done. He might even send me home, and Asa would agree with him. If I was going to be like Asa or Mr. Place, I was going to have to get serious and work a lot harder at growing up.

Chapter Eight

In September, we returned to school for our senior year. I again rode the school bus, for even though I'd earned some money working for Mr. Place, I didn't earn enough to buy a car. Whitey Carlson never paid me for building the fence and painting the barn, for which I couldn't blame him, and I wasn't about to go and ask for it. Also, I had the feeling that Asa didn't really want me to have a car just then anyway, so I didn't push it. I knew everybody else would have one, or a pickup at least, and we'd all had licenses since we were fifteen, except Hetty, who couldn't get one. I was content to let things occur naturally, content to be just a kid for a while longer without the responsibility of owning my own car.

Just before school started, I did make one trip out to Carlson's place to visit the site of my disaster. With the exception of my fence and the two outbuildings, the place was empty, the trailer gone along with Whitey and Donna.

The mobile home space was bare. Now that the ground was exposed, the bunch grass was already beginning to grow there. I walked the length of the empty spot, listening for I didn't know what, trying to feel something that was impossible to feel. As I walked the fence line it was puzzling to me that I wanted to see Donna one more time, for what reason I wasn't sure. I stopped to read the "Sold" sign stapled to the fence. A phone number was written along the bottom of the sign, and I realized that I could reach Donna by calling the number, though I knew I would never make the call, didn't really want to make it.

I climbed up and straddled the top rail, looked at the barn and the tack shed, then shifted and looked again at the space where the trailer house had been. I sat for maybe fifteen minutes considering the events that had taken place there. It was like watching scenes from a movie reviewing my immediate past. I was surprised that I had fallen so easily, surprised that I had been more than willing to close my eyes to the good judgment Asa and Lydia had tried to instill in me. I'd focused only on the seduction I had imagined and blocked out everything else I cared for, everything I'd been taught about being a good human being. I just flat hadn't cared that I was with another man's wife, and I never really considered the consequences. I climbed down from the fence and walked back into Powder River, feeling that I had closed a book I didn't need to finish reading. I never again went out to the site.

The morning of September 6th, with an early fall clearly in the air; I walked from the house, through Hyatt's General store, where I bought two pencils and a spiral notebook, down the road past the Powder River School and the church, to the Swede's Shell Station. I went early so I could stand alone with my thoughts for a while before any of the others arrived.

I needed time to prepare myself for the voices and the faces of my bus mates. I wanted to re-enter the mainstream of their world slowly, for once we stepped on to the yellow and black bus, it would be wild and raucous, what with kids excited about seeing one another after the long summer. It had certainly been the longest summer of my life, a summer that had really begun in April when Lydia walked out on us.

I knew Hetty was thrilled about being a senior. She'd spoken of it throughout August. I was neither excited, nor unexcited. I was looking forward to the change of scenery, but that's about all. One thing I was not looking forward to was making a decision about what I was going to do after graduation. I just didn't want to think about it.

I know that not long after our arrival, the pressure would begin with teachers asking, *What are you going to do after graduation? Are you going to school, or are you going to work?* And we'd all have to meet with the college counselor. College counseling consisted of trying to enroll us for our first two years at Casper Jr. College or the University of Wyoming, and the more conservative thinkers would encourage us to attend Chadron State Teachers College in Chadron, Nebraska. The counselor always tried to get someone enrolled at Yale, Harvard or Stanford, but I don't believe anyone was ever accepted, though in retrospect someone must have been accepted occasionally.

But that first back-to-school morning, wearing polished cowboy boots, jeans, denim jacket and a new, plaid shirt, I stood alone at the bus stop for about half-an-hour, my shoulders hunched against the cool air. I faced the rising sun until it warmed the front half of my body, then turned my back to it and warmed the other half.

Ole Andersson, big and blond, wearing coveralls, came out to me. He held two cups of coffee.

"Back to school?"

"Yep. Senior year."

He smiled and handed me a cup. "Coffee?"

"Sure, Ole. Thanks."

"You're early this morning Matthew. Want to come inside?"

"No thanks, Ole. It's nice out here, and soon it'll be too cold to stand out here early."

"Yah! Soon enough," he said. "Matthew? If you want a part-time job, I could use someone after school and on Saturdays. I'll pay a dollar twenty-five an hour."

"Oh! Sounds good. I certainly could use the money, and it'll keep me out of trouble."

Our eyes met, and I laughed a sheepish laugh. He chuckled. "Yah! We've all had enough trouble to go around."

"It's a deal then?" he asked, offering his hand.

"It is." I said, tucking my notebook under my arm, taking his hand and giving it a good, strong shake.

"I'll start today after school, if that's fine."

"Sure," he said.

"You know the bus doesn't get back until about four."

"That's good. You can work from four to six and all day Saturday. See you later." And he turned and went back inside.

I stood alone for a few minutes more, appreciating the silence and the coffee before I saw Tommy Svareland walking toward me. I hadn't seen him since early summer, and he'd grown and changed some. He was taller, and his face was longer. I raised my cup to him and he returned my greeting as he picked up his pace to join me at the bus stop.

He had a man's face really, and looking at him I realized that we were all men now, young men to be sure, but no longer boys.

"Hi, Matt," he said, "How are you?"

"I'm okay, I guess. How about you, Tommy?"

"I'm fine, but call me Tom now. I'm having everybody call me Tom."

"Sounds about right," I told him.

"Well, you can't be a kid forever."

"No you can't," I responded. "How are your grandmother and Clive?"

"Good. They're both good. How are your folks? They gonna get back together?"

"No, I don't think they'll ever get back together; but they're fine."

"How's Lucky?"

"Still lucky I guess."

Adriana Hudson and Ernie Clasp arrived together, walking from the south on the road to Place's ranch. Adriana was wearing Ernie's school ring on a chain around her neck. They'd started going steady over the summer. Later they would marry and live outside of Powder River on a small subsistence ranch that would make them a simple living as long as he worked a day job. They would spend the rest of their lives in Powder River.

Hetty was the last to arrive, her father dropping her off in the pickup I had driven through August. The kids at the bus stop were impressed with Hetty's new look, her hair more styled, her makeup and her new glasses. Everyone was wearing something new: glasses, shirts, skirts, jeans, and I sported a somewhat crooked nose. Like Tom Svareland, we all looked older, not at all the kids we were in the spring. I did wonder how I looked to them and what they thought of me and my summer debacle.

Once we boarded the bus and picked up the Natrona kids, the talk got serious. All kinds of stories had to be told, news of happenings that kids had saved throughout the summer and stored up for this very moment. It was a kind of disorganized reunion with everybody getting their chance to talk. A Natrona kid named Miller started it off.

"Did you hear that Larry Packer shot his brother's eye out while rabbit hunting?"

"Really?"

"Yeah, they were hunting just west of that old tank farm near Casper and they ran a rabbit into a pipe. Larry and his brother, Steve, were at opposite ends of the pipe, and Steve had Larry rattle his rifle around and around at his end to drive the rabbit out. Steve put his head to the ground to see the rabbit huddled in the middle of the pipe and told Larry to bang the end of the pipe with his rifle. Anyway, Larry's rifle went off and the bullet spiraled around the rabbit and hit Steve in the eye."

"Wow!"

"Oh, man!"

"Which eye?"

"Did he lose his eye?"

"Hell yes, he lost his eye. Larry shot it out. I just told you. It would have been worse if the slug hadn't spent a lot of its energy spiraling around in the pipe. Brain damage, maybe if not dead."

"He's got a glass eye. I've seen it. It's blue, just like his other eye, but you can tell right off it ain't real. It looks kind of like a marble, a cat's eye. But it looks okay. Larry says Steve takes it out and rinses it at the sink."

The talk went on the whole trip to the high school; ranch kids talking about ranch problems, cattle with Bangs Disease, hay that had burned up with their daddy's barn, horses that hit barbed wire fences and ripped open their shoulders. Hetty changed her mind about keeping our secret and told them the rattlesnake story. And I, well I did not talk about Donna and Whitey Carlson, and to my great relief, nobody asked.

We learned that Bud Marby, a city kid, drowned in a reservoir east of Casper. He and another guy had gone diving with air tanks and had wrapped lengths of chain around the tanks to allow them to walk on the bottom. Bud ran out of oxygen and couldn't get back up. His friend got panicky and rose to the surface, swam to shore and tried to get help from a nearby ranch house, but by the time they got back and were able to bring him up, which took a long time because of the chains, he was dead. So we rode to school that first day catching up on all the news, and wondered which classes and which teachers we would have to endure. All in all I was glad to be back, to be around lots of people again after my summer in Powder River.

After the school day was over the talk on the bus on the way home was all about teachers, assignments, new kids at the school, and the upcoming football season, the events of summer no longer our focus. When we got to Powder River, I walked into Ole's Shell Station and put in two hours of work, content to be back in school and working for Ole.

It turned out to be an enjoyable fall. School and work put me on a steady course and an even keel, and Asa and I developed a nice routine and closer relationship. We got into the habit of driving into Casper most Sundays to attend a church there, as Asa had resigned from piano playing at the Powder River church. He knew I was uncomfortable there, and the truth was that without Lydia he wasn't exactly comfortable himself, so we found an American Lutheran church at the corner of 7th and Durbin. Asa liked the minister, a "real down-to-earth guy," whose name was Larson.

After church we'd go on over to the Saddle Rock Café and have dinner, where Asa and I talked about his past and my future. We got to know one another differently, and I felt we were just two men sharing our lives. It was during one of those Sunday afternoon talks that I began to think about being a lawyer, and events later in the year only advanced that thought.

In addition to our new Sunday routine, we began to drive up to Thermopolis to swim in the Star Plunge. Thermopolis had natural hot springs, and two pools provided swimming, the Star Plunge and the Washaki. We'd soak and swim in the hot, soothing waters, enjoying the early fall weather. It was a fun time, and I wondered why we never went up there in all the years my mother lived with us.

The drive was only about a hundred and thirty miles, first west to Shoshone, then north on highway 20 to Thermopolis. It was scenic, as Wyoming highways go, especially through Wind River Canyon, with the Big Horn River churning and boiling over the rocks with the steep walls of the canyon on either side. The highway was carved out right next to the river, and if you imagined just a little, you felt you were on the water shooting the rapids at great speed.

On the way home we'd stop at the Dam Bar and Café just south of Boysen Reservoir to have dinner. The Dam Bar had the men and ladies' rooms across the highway from the restaurant, so folks had to walk across the highway to use them. On the door to the men's rooms it said, "Pointers," and on the door to the women's room it said, "Setters," which I found funny. According to the women who used the ladies' room, there was a tape recording triggered by pressure on the toilet seat, and when a woman sat down a voice called out, "Be careful, lady, we're working down here."

One Sunday even as we returned after dark, the sky was heavy with clouds. It was just about cold enough to snow, being late October. We had just left the Dam Bar and were still along the Big Horn just out of the canyon when lightning struck a barbed wire fence along the highway. Asa stopped the truck immediately, and we rolled down the windows. The lightning hit the fence and traveled along it, casting a blue, sparking glow. It traveled for about an eighth of a mile crackling and arcing, burning the tops of the fence posts. It was eerie, like God sending a message to Moses, and as suddenly as it had struck; it disappeared, leaving only the bright blue image on our eyelids when we blinked. Then the wind picked up and it began to rain heavy drops mixed with snow.

"I saw that once before when I was a kid," Asa began.

"I was in a barn loft with another kid watching it rain, and the lightning struck his fence, lighting up the barnyard for about thirty seconds. It's a rare sight alright."

I felt lucky to have seen it, and seeing it with Asa made it that much more special.

Really cold weather arrived with Halloween, accompanied by the usual pranks. The lower temperatures seemed to bring out the devil in us. A bunch of guys stole an outhouse and stood it on the lawn in front of Natrona County High School. Some others killed four chickens and hung them from the trees around the school.

While we were inside the gym where the dance was held, a couple of the boys discovered that one of the English teachers, Mr. Schell, who had just bought a new 1957 Volkswagen Beetle, had left it parked in the parking lot near the gym door, unlocked with the key in the ignition. They started it up and drove it directly in front of the big, double doors, so close that the doors couldn't be opened enough for people to pass through. Then they locked the keys in the car. We all had to exit through the hallway and out another door. They had to call a locksmith to open up the car before Mr. Schell could drive it away.

The principal and teachers did not find the pranks funny at all. I thought the outhouse was great, but agreed with them about the chickens and Mr. Schell's car. They never discovered who did it. The culprits and their friends were exceptionally tight lipped, and even weeks later when we asked someone, "Who did it?" They just winked and ran their finger over their mouths, zipping their lips closed.

But the Halloween dance at the high school wasn't the only place to suffer Halloween pranks. Without telling a soul, Ernie Clasp and Adriana Hudson left the Halloween dance early and drove back to Powder River to let the air out of dozens of tires in front of the American Legion Hall, where folks were dancing and drinking. The mood of the townspeople was plain dangerous when they discovered it. Had they caught the culprits they would have done mayhem if not murder.

Of course, not all of the adults were upset about it. Some were too drunk to notice. Others kept the Halloween party going until morning, and then walked over to the Tumble Inn for a big breakfast before having me pump up their tires and driving home. Some slept in their vehicles, waking stiff and cold, and a few used the occasion to shack up.

Saturday morning, November 1st, I walked from the house down to the service station. Swede trusted me to open up the place. Along the road I saw a number of broken Jack O' Lanterns, their partial faces looking macabre. And of course, there were still a number of cars and pickups parked around the Legion Hall with their tires flat, so I fired up the big Chevy truck of Ole's, the one with the generator and air compressor on it, and pumped up the rest of the tires for the folks. They were grateful and tipped generously, and my work freed me of suspicion.

Parents questioned their kids for a week, but no one seemed to know who'd done it. Asa asked me about it, but I was at the high school in Casper and never heard a word until morning. The younger kids were at a party at the Powder River school bobbing for apples. Since all the kids seemed to be accounted for, the adults began to suspect one another and everybody was distrustful for a week or so. I finally learned it was Ernie and Adriana the next summer while serving as best man for their wedding.

We had two fairly light snowfalls the first week of November, but nothing serious. The mornings were pretty cold, of course, always below freezing, and the wind blew sharply against our faces while we stood at the bus stop each morning. Gloves and hats had become common apparel, and I'd taken to wearing a sheepskin-lined, leather jacket I'd bought from Clive Svareland for thirty-five dollars. It was too big for me, but I thought it looked cool, and it pleased me to be wearing a man's jacket.

Working for Swede was a great blessing to me, as I was pretty good with numbers and it was easy to handle all sales and repair transactions. I also liked working on cars and trucks, changing oil and oil filters, lubing and tuning up. Most Saturdays I'd have my head under the hood of a pickup changing spark plugs, with the radio tuned to KVOC or KTWO, humming along with fats Domino or maybe Marty Robbins. If I was in the mood for country music, I would sing along with Little Jimmy Dickens singing, "Sleeping at the Foot of the Bed," or "Take an Old Cold Tater and Wait."

On the 17th of November we got hammered with a major snowstorm with sixty mile an hour winds and blinding snow. The wind damaged mobile homes across the state and turned over trailer rigs in Powder River Pass between Ten Sleep and Buffalo, and up at Togwotee Pass near Moran Junction.

The weather service issued stockmen's warnings, and a number of ranchers dropped hay for their cattle and sheep before the storm actually hit. The bus didn't run for two days, and the Powder River and Natrona kids got an extra vacation in the middle of the week. Asa walked to the PO both days rather than take the pickup, but he had me start it each noon to guarantee its running. Temperatures ranged from five below at night to sixteen during the day, and the wind piled up five-foot drifts in places, blocking roads and causing havoc throughout the state. In the two-day blow we piled up fourteen inches of snow and the world turned white. Either frost or snow caked the sides of every building in town. For kids it was a great adventure, but most adults found it worrisome, as they had to keep cattle and sheep alive, mend frozen water pipes, and keep their families in groceries.

The sun broke clear on the third day, casting its reflection off the snow so brightly it hurt our eyes. The temperatures stayed low, and there wasn't any doubt that winter had arrived. I spent hours putting mud and snows on cars and pickups, and chaining folks up. We returned to school to discover that the city kids hadn't gotten the days off, and we walked tall boasting of our extra days to play.

Chapter Nine

Asa and I had Thanksgiving with the Betty and her folks rather than eat alone, as it was our first Thanksgiving without Lydia. Friday we both worked all day, and Saturday, when Asa closed the PO at noon, we agreed to meet at the Tumble Inn for lunch.

We walked down to the highway together, then parted, going in opposite directions. It was only twelve degrees with hard snow still covering the ground. It grew cloudy and we thought we might get another round of snow.

I worked until noon pumping gas and remounting snow tires. When Asa didn't come for lunch by twelve thirty, I figured he'd gotten busy with early Christmas mail or a freight shipment or something, so I decided to walk up and see if I could help him out as soon as Swede relieved me.

Walking up to the PO I half expected to see Asa walking in my direction, but I was the only one walking. My work boots squeaked on the hard-packed snow. I enjoyed the sound and the rhythm of my footsteps. The wind forced me to hunch my shoulders and I pulled my stocking cap down over my ears. Traffic was nonexistent, as most people remained indoors, what with it being Thanksgiving weekend and all.

As I approached the Post Office, I was aware that there weren't any cars parked in front, and when I tried the front door it was locked. I peered through the window, but could only see the counter, the bank of shiny brass doors to the mail boxes, and the doorway into the back room. I thought Asa had probably just locked up and was still tidying up in the back, so I walked around the building and entered through the back door.

"Asa?" I called out, without receiving a reply.

"Asa?" I called again, apprehensive now, and stepped through the door leading into the front of the Post Office, where Asa usually sat behind the counter on a tall wooden stool. He was sprawled on the floor on his back, the stool on the floor beside him with his left arm caught in the legs of the stool, his shirt-front soaked in blood. My breath caught, and I felt a surge of fear rise up as I dropped to him and cradled him in my arms. His eyes, wide with his own fright captured me.

"I've been shot in the chest, and I think I might die," is what he whispered to me.

It was strange how it played in my head. I thought of the words to, *The Streets of Laredo*, in which the cowboy says, "I'm shot in the chest and I'm dying today."

It's crazy I know, but the melody played even as I dialed Swede's number at the service station with Asa lying at my feet, his life's blood filling his shirt and on the floor now too, and on my hands and arms from when I held him.

"Swede! Dad's been shot! Help me! My God, he's gonna die! I'm at the P.O. Hurry!"

It didn't sound like my voice. It sounded too high, like the voice of a little boy who didn't know what to do, which is what you become, I guess, when you find your father shot and bleeding on the floor.

I hadn't referred to Asa as Dad since I was about eight years old, and it didn't even register that I had done so until later when I was sitting in the surgery waiting room with Swede and Lydia.

The drawback to living in Powder River was that it had no doctor. There wasn't a clinic, or even a vet. When emergencies occurred there was always a thirty-eight-mile wild ride into Casper. Ranchers and their kids, cowboys and pregnant women were all rushed in a pickup or a passenger car to Natrona County Memorial Hospital. Some of them bled to death along the way, or their appendix burst before they arrived. Most pregnant women had the foresight to go to Casper early, or counted on having their babies at home.

Immediately after I called Swede, I called the Sheriff's office in Casper. Swede told me to inform them that we'd be on our way in his Jeep station wagon. By the time I hung up, he was at the back door, and we carefully picked Asa up and slid him into the back of the wagon. I cradled his head in my lap. He was no longer conscious, his face was pale and his breathing shallow and foamy. I feared he would die before we could get to Casper; so as we drove, careening over icy roads, Swede and I recited a chant to keep him alive.

"Easy now, Asa. Just take it easy now," Swede spoke over his shoulder while alternately my voice encouraged, "It's all right, Asa. You're going to be all right." It was as if our voices could hold him together, could slow the flow of blood that was pumping out of him.

Despite risky road conditions, Swede drove like a drunken cowboy, the four-wheel drive Jeep throwing snow where it had drifted over the highway, skidding and swerving when he hit hard packed snow. Swede drove with his lights on, leaning on the horn whenever he passed traffic, which fortunately wasn't often. Most folks were indoors eating leftover turkey.

Our prayer changed slightly.

"Don't let him die. Dear God, don't let him die."

"Easy now Asa; just a little longer. Take it easy now."

"It's gonna be all right, Asa. You're gonna be all right."

"Don't let him die. Dear God, don't let him die."

The Sheriff's car picked us up just the other side of Natrona. He swung around when he saw us, and Swede slowed down a bit until the patrol car passed us and then both cars continued speeding toward Casper on our life-saving mission, the sheriff's siren and flashing lights adding to the sense of urgency.

I was in shock, and too scared to cry, feeling as if my world was ending. I felt disoriented and tried to help Asa by sheer will, holding him tightly as if trying to keep his life from getting away from me. If I held him tightly enough, he would live. They had to force my fingers from their grip when we arrived at the hospital, and they later discovered bruises on Asa's upper arms where I'd gripped him so tightly on the long ride into town.

The arrival was chaotic it seemed to me, yet the emergency crew was at the door of the ER, lifesaving equipment already in place. They forced Asa from my arms and bound him to a stretcher, gentleness not a consideration at the moment. The lights of the sheriff's car continued to flash while voices barked out sharp orders and responses, and I was pushed aside while Asa was taken away. Swede and I stood helplessly against the corridor wall as Asa disappeared into an elevator. I knew I'd not see him alive again.

With Asa gone I realized the other emergency room patrons were watching us, wide-eyed, trying not to panic after the scene they had just witnessed. A nurse led us into another elevator and took us up to surgery waiting.

"Would you like a cup of coffee?" she asked, as if nothing serious were happening.

"No thanks," Swede answered, "but if you had a little whiskey, I could sure stand a drink."

She smiled disapprovingly and left us in the company of an old, gnarled cowboy in faded jeans and a western shirt, his cowboy hat still on his head. He stood up and pulled a flask from his hip pocket. Handing it to Swede, he said, "Helps a bit."

Swede drank, then handed the flask to me. I took a swallow. It was thick and bitter, but I drank it, though it burned all the way down and I coughed up a brief storm.

"Much obliged," Swede said, wiping his hand over the lip of the flask before returning it. The cowboy took a swig of his own and capped the flask before sliding it back into his jeans.

"His daddy's been shot," Swede said. "In Powder River."

"Son of a bitch," the cowboy said, and sat down abruptly.

I had to call Lydia, so found a telephone on a counter, the sign on which read, "Local Calls Only." It rang three times before she picked up the receiver.

"Hello?"

Suddenly I couldn't get the words out. "Hello?"

"Mother, it's Matthew."

She could hear in my voice the words I was unable to say. "What's happened?" she asked. "What's happened to Asa?"

"He's been shot in the chest. It's awful bad. We're at the hospital. Swede is here. He brought us in. Can you come?"

"Oh, my Lord," she said. "I'll be there, Matthew. I'll be right there."

So we began our vigil, my mother, Swede and me, a vigil which lasted five hours originally, then days, before we knew that Asa would live.

Hospital waiting rooms are really ante-rooms to Hell. They smack of death. In a waiting room, people speak either too loud or too soft. A television flashes unreal images into the room, images of people smiling and laughing, or maybe singing. The odor of the room was a blend of disinfectant cleaner, hospital food and cigarette smoke.

Sometime during the wait, the sheriff's deputy came up and we all three accompanied him into the hall, where he questioned me about my discovery. I could only relay how I found my father.

The deputy informed us that they'd gone over the Post Office, but couldn't tell whether anything had been taken. It didn't look like robbery, as no drawers had been turned out and the place wasn't ransacked. The small amount of money Asa kept in a drawer from stamp and envelope sales was still there. If Asa lived, he alone would be able to tell us what happened.

We continued our wait, drinking cokes and coffee, and eating tasteless sandwiches. Numbness set in, that merciful numbness that allowed us to ignore the heartfelt pain and the paralyzing fear of death. We spoke little, sitting up with sudden anticipation whenever a weary doctor came into view, or when a nurse called for someone in the waiting room. We prayed of course, always silently, privately, but sometimes our lips moved with our words, and it was clear to me that both Swede's and my mother's prayers matched my plea for God to keep my father alive. I'd found Asa about 12:40, and it wasn't until 6:45 that a doctor we'd never seen before stepped into the waiting room and called our name.

"Christman?"

The three of us rose and followed him into the hall.

"I'm Doctor Redmond. I've completed surgery on Mr. Christman. You're his wife?"

"Yes," Lydia replied, and I didn't argue the point.

The doctor's eyes were red. His hair messed, and Asa's blood splattered his green smock. He kept running his hand over his face as if to wipe away cobwebs.

"Mr. Christman was shot in the chest with a .38 caliber handgun. The bullet entered the right side of his chest, slightly to the right of center, missing the aorta and the heart, but not by much. It shattered two ribs going in and lodged at the back of the rib cage. We were able to remove the slug successfully."

"Thank God," my mother said.

"He's lost a great deal of blood, much of it before we ever got to work on him; and of course, he lost more while we worked. He needs a transfusion. Are any of you his blood type?"

"Matthew is," Lydia told him, which was news to me.

"We'll take some blood then, and the sooner the better."

"Is he going to die?" I asked.

"I don't know yet."

"When will you know?" I pressed anxiously.

"Maybe tomorrow; maybe not until the next day. He's in a coma. His body has suffered severe trauma. I don't know if he is strong enough to weather it. Now, let's get some blood."

A short time later they took my blood. I don't know how much, but it seemed like a lot. I didn't mind. I knew that I could help Asa by giving it. I felt good being able to do something at last, something other than praying. He would have my blood coursing through his veins, just as I had his coursing through mine. I knew it was all up to God, but I also knew my blood might help save him.

After we returned to the waiting room, I found myself confused that the doctor didn't know whether or not Asa would live. It seemed to me that the doctor should know. He was the doctor, wasn't he? He was, after all, trained to do the work. Doctors were mysterious to me, almost like gods. They held great power. They made a lot of money. Certainly, it seemed to me, he should know whether or not Asa was going to recover.

I compared doctors to auto mechanics, since I'd been working on cars recently. When I tuned a car or a pickup, I knew it would run. When I fixed a flat, I knew it would hold air.

And yet, to be honest, I knew that I'd tuned cars that never ran smoothly, and I didn't have the slightest idea why. No matter how much I adjusted the timing or the carburetor, replaced plugs, set the points; no matter how well I did it all, some cars just wouldn't run smoothly. When necessary I'd have Swede come in and check it all out for me; and after a test drive he would declare it tuned, only to have it stutter and balk when the owner picked it up. Still, cars were not people, and I thought a doctor should be able to tell whether his work was going to be successful or not.

After Asa was returned to his room and we finally got to see him, I almost didn't recognize him. For a second I thought he was already dead, and I wished I had waited in the hall and let Lydia go in by herself.

His face was pasty white, his eyes closed, and what hair he did have was so matted I felt bad for him and wanted to comb it. He looked thin and terribly old. He had a white, plastic tube taped in his mouth, which ran to a respirator to aid his painful and labored breathing. His wounded chest rose and fell rhythmically, almost independently of Asa himself. Up down, up down, Wheeze Swoosh, Wheeze Swoosh, like that, with a mechanical click at each interval. He had an IV in his right arm, and my blood dripped through another plastic tube into his veins.

My mother squeezed his hand and asked him if he could hear her, if he knew who she was. He didn't respond. I too took hold of his hand and felt for a responsive squeeze, but he didn't return the pressure or blink, or nod, or smile like they always did in the movies to tell us they were going to live. No music rose in crescendo. The sun didn't suddenly shine through the window. Asa just lay there, and I feared he would die. I wanted so badly to tell him that I loved him before it happened, but I didn't have the courage or the where-with-all to do so.

Even though my mother and I were his family, we were only allowed to stay a few minutes that first visit, and frankly, I was glad I didn't have to stand there and look at him.

Lydia, Swede and I were directed to another waiting room on Asa's floor, where none of us spoke for a while, each preferring to be alone with our individual fears and prayers.

After a short time, Swede departed. He had to get back to the station and close it up properly, and he also spread the news in Powder River. I asked him to take care of Lucky, and he said he would feed him, see that he had water and let him out a couple times a day.

My mother and I stayed at the hospital until eleven that night, checking on Asa a couple of times an hour until we were so tired that we began to fall asleep in our chairs. Finally a nurse suggested we go home. She would call if we were needed. So Lydia drove us to her apartment in our old Buick. We collapsed in exhaustion and slept like the dead until morning, she in her bedroom and me on the sofa in her living room. I never undressed even, but didn't realize it until morning. We didn't receive any phone calls in the night, so knew Asa was still alive. No crisis had occurred that required our sleep to be shattered with the frightening ring in the dark vacuum of night.

I was hopeful, of course, that Asa would be awake when we arrived at the hospital, but that wasn't the case. He lay in his coma for five days. My mother and I spent the time praying, reading paperbacks, magazines and newspapers. We stared out the hospital windows at the bare park across the street, noting the dormant trees of winter and the beginning of a new snowfall, which added to the shroud already covering the frozen ground. We watched other people's faces register joy or pain as those around Asa recovered or died.

We alternated time at the hospital. Lydia would often let me sleep in and go up in the mornings. I often sat alone in the afternoons, allowing Lydia to get a nap and take care of personal business. We always had dinner at her apartment, which was a treat to me even under those conditions.

In the evenings she sang at the Gladstone Hotel, and I marveled at her ability to be so worried about Asa and still go out there and sing well at night. I made mention of it once, and she just smiled and said, "That's show business," jokingly, as if she were a Hollywood star.

The morning of the fifth day, Lydia went alone and found Asa awake. She called me immediately. I showered, washed and combed my hair, and put on a clean shirt before going up to the hospital. I wanted to look good for Asa's first morning back among the living. In my youth and excitement, I imagined him sitting up, taking broth, smiling and chattering. The truth was that he was only awake.

When I arrived, he no longer looked dead, but he didn't exactly look alive either. I wondered if maybe that was the way Lazarus looked the day Jesus called him out of his tomb. Asa lay on his back, his bed cranked up slightly. He was off the respirator, and the IV in his arm now fed him glucose and medication rather than my blood. I felt pleased and grateful that my blood had worked. He did smile at me and returned the squeeze I gave his hand, but he was weak, and his hello was only faintly whispered. He was unshaven, and clearly the worse for wear, but he was alive and likely to remain so. He would recover slowly until he was the old Asa who worked at the PO in Powder River, scratched the dog, and visited with me about my future. I could hardly wait to get him home.

I felt as if we'd all been granted new life, not only Asa, but Lydia and me as well, and for a few hopeful moments I believed my mother would give up singing at the Gladstone and return to Powder River to take care of us once again. It was a silly thought, I suppose, but a natural one, a thought I had from time to time until Lydia moved to Denver and remarried.

By the time I got Asa home, there were only two and a half weeks left before Christmas, so I stayed home from school to help Asa recover. I fixed his meals, helped him to take a bath and those sorts of things.

I picked up my books and assignments at the high school before we returned to Powder River. Since it was so close to Christmas the teachers were more than amenable to it. The women teachers clucked sympathetically. Miss Dirkson actually hugged and kissed me on the cheek. I looked into her eyes in search of desire, but I only saw kindness. The men teachers slapped me on the back and shook my hand, reminding me to be strong.

Tending Asa made me more aware of his mortality, and I realized for the first time that someday I'd live a portion of my life without him in it. It was not an experience I was looking forward to having. We live for a long while as children believing our parents to be invincible, able to take care of every problem we bring to them. Then somewhere along the line they become human, vulnerable, flawed. My mother became fully human for me the day she left, my father the day he was shot in the chest.

Another startling lesson I learned through Asa's wounding was that I too would die someday. It was a thing I'd known only intellectually, but as I tended Asa I realized that death had actually become a reality for me. A grim reaper who smiled his white, skeletal smile and motioned with a bony finger for me to follow really did exist. I'd been lucky in the past. I could have been snake-bit that day with Hetty, or lost my foot and bled to death while playing with bear traps out at Rutterman's. Whitey could have beaten me to death. Even the day of the beating I never thought about dying. While it was going on, I just wanted him to stop, and afterwards I was just glad it was over. We always know the fact of death, but don't know the power of it until it strikes close to home. No, I never grasped death's meaning until the afternoon I found Asa on the Post Office floor.

Twice in the first two weeks a highway patrolman and the sheriff came to the house to speak with Asa, but he wasn't able to be helpful. He only remembered a man he didn't recognize entering the PO, but not the shooting or any words exchanged.

The sheriff said they'd interrogated a couple of drifters without evidence they might have been the shooter. The highway patrolman arrested a man between Shoshone and Riverton who'd stolen a pickup in front of a diner, but he clearly wasn't in or near Powder River at the time. His estranged wife corroborated his story of his whereabouts. In short, Asa's assailant was never found.

One night, a week or so after we'd brought Asa home, somebody knocked at our front door. People had been dropping by to see Asa since his arrival, and I assumed it was probably Mr. Place or Clive, or maybe the Reverend Henderson. Asa was sitting up in bed reading a magazine. I was sitting on the floor of his room near the wall heater trying to pay attention to some of the school work I'd brought home. I placed my book on the floor and went to the door, and when I opened it, Whitey Carlson stood before me, uncomfortably rolling the brim of his cowboy hat in his hands.

"I hear Asa's been shot," he said softly. "I come to see him."

Nothing could have surprised me more, and I was both frightened and embarrassed that he had come. I knew there was no reason to be frightened, but it was the first time I'd seen Whitey since summer, and it brought back such painful memories that I didn't know what to say. I stood before him speechless, my left hand on the doorknob, the December wind sweeping into the house. I'm not sure which of us was more uncomfortable.

"If he's asleep I wouldn't want to bother him. You just tell him I called," he said finally, and began to turn away.

"No, he's awake. Come on in. He's in there," I said, pointing to the door of Asa's bedroom.

I watched the back of his sheepskin jacket as he moved away from me, then I stood with the front door wide open, wondering if Donna were waiting for him in his truck. I stepped out into the cold night to look, but saw only an empty pickup, and heard the engine ticking under the hood as it cooled in the cold winter night.

I returned to the living room, closing the door and listening to their voices in the Asa's room. I didn't join them, but went to my own room and sat on the bed. Only about ten minutes passed before I heard Whitey's footsteps cross the wood floor, heard the door opening and closing, heard his truck start up and drive away. It was only then that I went back into Asa's room.

"What did he want?" I asked angrily.

"He wanted to know how I was," Asa answered. "Whitey and I been friends a lot of years."

I knew that to be the truth, and remembered Whitey saying to me the day he hired me that he'd always liked Asa.

"And he give me this for you," Asa continued, handing me a roll of bills.

"It's the pay for building the fence and painting the barn. He says you earned it, and he shoulda give it to you before…and he said Donna left him."

"She left him?" I responded, shocked.

"Yep. Run off with a rodeo hand from Billings in October. Whitey's alone on that spread up in the Big Horns now."

I reached out and took the rolled-up bills and counted them.

"He's left $300. I can't believe he'd pay me after…well, after what I did."

"Well, Whitey did agree to pay you when he hired you…He's a lot of things, Whitey is, but he's a man of his word where work is concerned. I'm sure he forgot in all the ruckus, and for a while he probably didn't think you deserved it, what with carrying on with his wife the way you did. And now, of course, she's gone, and he knows it wasn't all your fault. Now that he's been rejected, he's been made a fool of twice over by that woman. Looks like she made fools out of the both of you. He's finally learned what many of us suspected all along. She was just no good."

I didn't like hearing it, and didn't want to have any sympathy for Whitey, but I knew it to be the truth. The toughest truths to accept are the ones about ourselves, and I didn't want to know that Whitey and I were brother fools.

Whitey, it turned out, was just like the rest of the folks in Powder River. They could fight you, gossip about you, laugh at you, but if you were in trouble, they would help. Asa had been shot, and Whitey wanted Asa to know that they were friends, that he'd help Asa in whatever way possible. He showed respect for Asa by coming to see him and giving Asa the money I'd earned, but didn't deserve.

All of the Powder River people were good, strong, kind-hearted western stock, and they knew that one day they'd have trouble of their own; and when it came their neighbors would offer aid in one form or another. Since the day Asa returned home, I had hardly cooked a meal. They'd set up a telephone chain while Asa was still in the hospital, and every family accepted the responsibility of delivering a hot meal on a given day. I spent two weeks delivering platters and pans with people's last names taped to the lids, and Asa did something that Lydia used to do, something I'd never seen him do. He wrote thank you notes.

With Christmas approaching and money in my pocket, I decided to make what would have been a disastrous Christmas a particularly special one. I would buy my parents fine gifts, in addition to being responsible for the Christmas tree. So as soon as Tom Svareland and Hetty were out of school, we made plans to cut Christmas trees for our homes. We'd make a day of it, and maybe bring one back for the church and Legion Hall as well.

The Monday after their release from school, we loaded up Asa's pickup with fifty-pound sand bags for weight, firewood, blankets, axes, and an enormous lunch.

We followed highway 20 into Natrona where we stopped at the Natrona store and had coffee and donuts before dropping south toward Pine Mountain, elevation 6,722 feet. We'd picnicked there in the past, so knew the road well.

The county road was open much of the way up, so we were able to get a good spot where the young trees were thick and the snow not terribly deep. We built a raging fire with the firewood we'd brought along, supplementing it with gnarled greasewood. We'd cut one tree, then stand around the fire for a while before cutting another one, eating our lunch a bit at a time. All our food was gone before noon.

"We'd better cut an extra tree," Hetty suggested.

"For who?" Tom and I asked.

"You never know," she said. "There's always somebody you think of later."

"Such as?" I challenged.

"I don't know," Hetty said. "We'll know when we see them."

We thought she was a little crazy, but went ahead and cut another tree to throw in the pickup.

Tom produced a flask of whiskey Clive kept in a kitchen drawer, and we passed it around. Hetty choked on it, but not that much more than Tom or I did. We sang Jingle Bells and White Christmas much of the time, the words we knew anyway, which were never enough to complete a whole song, but the choruses were great. Because of Hetty's balance problems and the whiskey, she fell down in the snow a couple of times, but because she was with us, she only laughed and didn't seem embarrassed at all.

We gossiped about school mates and teachers, and talked about our plans for the fall after graduation. It was then they learned I wanted to be a lawyer. The man who'd shot Asa had never been caught, and that had really influenced my thinking. I wanted justice, and in my young idealism I felt that if I couldn't get justice for Asa, I could get it for others.

Since we'd eaten everything in our food stock, we were starved again by two o'clock, so covered the fire with snow, watching it sizzle, smoke and steam. Then we drove back to the Natrona store, where we each had a hamburger and fries, and where we left the extra tree.

"See! I told you it would come in handy. Weren't they just pleased?" Tom and I remained silent.

After filling up, we drove back to Powder River and dropped off the trees, one at the American Legion Hall and one at the church before driving to our place. Asa was pleased, and invited us in, so we all sat around jawing and drinking more hot coffee until Tom dragged his tree up the road to their house, and I ran Hetty out to the Place ranch and dropped her off with her tree.

Later, while soaking in a hot tub of water, I didn't want the day to end, so called to Asa, "Hey, Asa! Let me take you down to the Tumble Inn and treat you to a steak dinner. You wanna go down there?"

He walked slowly into the bathroom and sat down on the toilet seat. He still looked tired and a little washed out, but was pretty good considering.

"You should save that money for school," he said.

"I'm gonna spend this money for dinner and for your Christmas gift. Let's have a steak. Isn't red meat good for your blood?" he hesitated, but finally agreed.

From the time we entered the front door of the Tumble Inn, folks greeted Asa, welcoming him back among the living, shaking his hand and telling him how worried they'd been, and that their prayers had surely been answered. It helped him to be out and have people so happy to see him. It was different than being the convalescent and receiving visitors at home, where he was the sick one. It gave him confidence to be at the Tumble Inn, with its soft lighting and the jukebox blaring out country and western Christmas songs. It lifted his spirits and made him happy to be among his people once again.

The next night Asa watched as I put up the tree. He hung a few ornaments, but let me do the lights and any high work on a chair. The tree was a little too large for the room, because trees in the wild will fool you, surrounded as they are by so much space. When you get them home you discover how small a house really is, but the room was just big enough to accommodate it, and there were only two of us, so we cut the branches back a bit and kept it.

Lucky wouldn't leave it alone, however, and lifted his leg on it that same evening. I hit him with a rolled-up newspaper, but it was too late, of course, so the tree had a slightly pungent smell until I took it down.

Christmas Eve, Lydia drove out with presents. She had a wool shirt and three pair of socks for me, and a wool shirt and a pair of gloves for Asa. Asa hadn't bought her anything, but I had a scarf and a bottle of White Shoulders perfume for her. Hetty helped me pick it out.

We went to church and sat in the back, singing hymns and listening to the Christmas message that was one thousand, nine hundred and fifty-seven years old. It was a story we'd grown up with and believed, and which always added meaning to our lives. After the hard times we'd shared, it supported us and made us know that despite our flaws, we were loved, if imperfectly by one another, perfectly by God.

My mother drove home immediately after the service, as a heavy storm was predicted by morning. After she left, Asa and I exchanged gifts privately. It seemed more appropriate, having spent half of our year alone together. I bought him a book called, Arundel, by Kenneth Roberts, about the American Revolutionary War. Asa always loved war history. I also gave him a white cowboy hat. He said it was because he was one of the good guys.

He gave me a used, leather bound, two-volume set of Wyoming Law that he had Mr. Place find for me. He also gave me a white, Pendleton wool shirt.

Before we went to bed, we shared a rum and coke, and sat for a while looking at the tree in silence, feeling the camaraderie between a father and son that only comes occasionally in a lifetime.

Christmas morning, we woke to a blizzard; a four-day blow that piled up almost three feet of snow and shut down roads across the state. The wind howled relentlessly, blowing fine feather trails of snow through the chinks around the windows.

We'd planned to have Christmas dinner with the Places, but it really was too dangerous to go out, so Asa and I stayed home and had Christmas dinner ourselves. We'd gotten pretty comfortable with one another, and it was easy to do.

Asa took a leg of lamb out of the freezer, thawing it in water early on in the day. We boiled and mashed potatoes and opened some canned green beans put up by Tom's grandmother, and Asa baked us apples from some apples in the basement. It was as good a Christmas dinner as I'd ever eaten.

After dinner we listened to the radio while reading. I browsed through the law books, and Asa read a few chapters of Arundel. He fell asleep in his chair, his white cowboy hat on the back of his head, the book resting on his healing chest.

The wind continued its fury throughout the night, and an old locust tree banged its branches against the house, tapping out an irregular rhythm that began to sound like, God Rest Ye Merry Gentlemen as I dropped off to sleep.

The following morning, even with the wall heaters turned up high, we couldn't keep the house warm enough. All the windows were frosted with thick ice crystal patterns.

The storm raged, and we were completely house bound for three more days. We heard on the radio that a goodly number of sheep had piled up along fence lines and smothered trying to keep warm. There were highway deaths, and people were stranded across the state. Christmas travelers who couldn't reach home were put up in motels and restaurants along their route.

After the storm blew itself out, the temperatures dropped and stayed around twenty below zero, despite the bright hard sun that melted the frost on the windows only enough to change the crystal patterns.

The old year passed uneventfully. New Year's Eve was a quiet night for us. The cold snap still bore down, and although there was a New Year's Eve dance at the Legion Hall, we didn't go. Asa still tired easily, and the energy expended at a dance wasn't what he needed. We were content to read and listen on the radio for the world to usher in 1958. We heard later that dance turnout was low so they shut it down early.

At midnight we toasted one another with Cutty Sark and water. Since his return, Asa let me drink with him. It seemed that since we'd shared the worst of life and near death, we just as well share a drink together.

"Here's to your future," Asa offered, raising his glass. "And to yours," I countered, clicking his glass with mine.

"I came very close not to have one," he admitted, smiling thinly.

"I didn't think so either," I said. "And I wasn't looking forward to having one of my own without you, and you have Swede to thank."

"He's a good friend."

"Yes, he is."

"But you are my best friend," he said, bringing tears to both of our eyes.

"So, Happy New Year, Matthew."

"Happy New Year, Asa."

The drink, light on the scotch and heavy on the water, went down smoothly, warming my gullet, just as his words had warmed my heart. Then, tired and worn out by the events of 1957, Asa went to bed.

I sat up a while, pondering both my past and my future. I sincerely hoped I'd never have another year like the last one, too much trauma, too much pain. A guy can only walk close to the edge for so long before falling into the abyss. I'd been somewhat a rim-walker since the day my mother left, stayed at the precipice too long, and I wanted to move back to more solid ground with a horizon I could make out clearly and reach by day's end. I did feel awfully uncertain about 1958. I was looking forward to graduating, and I did want to start college and begin my quest to become a lawyer, but the thought of it all did overwhelm me.

I wanted to be on my own, maybe have an apartment in Laramie and work half-time while going to school, but I was somewhat afraid to leave Asa alone. His being shot made me want to stay around and protect him, made me want to check on him when I'd been away from the house too long. What if he never regained full strength? What if he needed me in the night? What if another guy entered the Post Office and shot him in the chest?

And, of course, I was afraid I might fail. What if I couldn't get through college, much less law school? No one on either side of my family had ever gone to college. I would be the first one. What if I wasn't bright enough to make it? I didn't want to come back to Powder River and take over for Asa or Swede, or even live under my father's roof, dependent and reclusive like some of the strange relatives I'd come across from the time I was young; silent and pale older brothers who peered out through living room curtains and left the ranch only at night to roam the countryside in bare feet. There was all that talk about sex with sheep. Not that I'd ever consider having sex with sheep, but the talk was there.

Despite my fears and uncertainties, I felt an excitement about meeting the unknown head on. After all, I was intelligent. I knew that. I'd always done well in school, and could talk and work with adults easily enough. Asa had reminded me often that every adult I knew had left his or her home and made a life in the world, people like Asa and Lydia, Swede and Mr. Place, even Clive Svareland, and I knew I was brighter than he was by a long shot. So, deep in my heart I knew I'd be all right; but that night, after the last sunset of 1957 and before the first dawn of 1958 would break over the frozen, snow-covered ground of Powder River, my thoughts about success and failure tossed back and forth until I finally gave up the ghost and went to bed.

Asa went back to work half-days about mid-January. He worked mornings and dropped me off at the bus stop before going on to the PO. He went home in the afternoons and took long naps, and it wasn't long before he gained some weight back and his energy level returned to normal.

I was pleased to be back in school and working for Swede, and it was fun to be with Hetty and the other seniors as we approached our last semester of high school. We would be out of school by mid-June, and we all knew that never again would we have to enter another classroom unless we chose to do so voluntarily.

Once in a while I stayed at Lydia's apartment on a Friday to go to a movie with the guys or attend a basketball game and dance at the school, but mostly I went home to Powder River, reluctant to leave Asa alone for the whole weekend.

In the late fall and winter the ride home from school always occurred in the dark, and I used to sit in the front so I could see the hundreds of jack rabbits and cottontails that would streak across the highway in the lights of the bus. If they didn't look, we hardly ever hit them, but there were always those who got blinded by the headlights and froze in the road until we went over them with a thump and a bump. The bus passed over a great many of them without touching them, of course, but a number always got flattened. Rabbit cakes, Hetty called them.

Once, after the driver let us off in Powder River, the bus hit a horse between Powder River and Waltman, killing the horse and sending the bus into the barrow pit. Fortunately, it didn't roll, and none of the remaining kids or the bus driver were seriously hurt, which made it a good story to tell for weeks afterwards.

About the time Asa returned to work, Lucky began to kill chickens. I discovered feathers and remains in the side-yard one Saturday morning. I also discovered the hole under the fence where he'd dug his way out. The chicken belonged to a Frenchman name Louvet, who lived about a quarter of a mile west of Powder River school along a dirt road. Louvet didn't know at first that Lucky was the culprit, and we chose not to tell him immediately. Asa wanted to try an old country remedy first.

He killed a chicken he bought from Tom Svareland's grandmother, and taped it around the dog's neck, up high where Lucky couldn't paw it off. Then we roped him in the yard. For a week, Lucky rolled in the snow, scratched at the chicken, rubbed against the fence trying to tear it off. He got mean and irritable, snapping at both Asa and me. The dead meat and the blood smell was awful, and we were sure it would cure the dog of his bad habits, but after Asa cut the chicken away, Lucky only went a week before he killed again. So Asa paid Louvet for the dead chickens, telling him we'd either get rid of the dog or chain him up, but we didn't have the heart to do either.

Late in January I couldn't find him anywhere. I walked down the road to Louvet's, but I didn't see Lucky at all. That evening I whistled and called from the door of the house, but he never showed up. He didn't come home that night at all, and I suspected that Louvet had shot him and buried him somewhere.

The next evening Clive Svareland found Lucky while doing some rabbit hunting with a flashlight. He knocked on our door, and when Asa opened it, there was Clive with the dog lying stiffly in his arms. We brought him in and examined him, but found no gunshot wounds. Asa felt Lucky's body to see if maybe he'd been hit by a car, but found nothing. Probably, he'd been poisoned. Lots of ranchers put out poisoned meat to kill varmints. It was illegal, but they did it anyway. Louvet probably set out poisoned bait, although we could never prove it, and in fairness to him, Lucky could have gotten his meat most anywhere around Powder River.

"Poor little guy," Clive sympathized. "His luck just plain run out."

"I guess," was all that I could say.

We wrapped the dog in some burlap sacks and set him outside until morning, when we used a pick to break through a foot of frozen ground before hitting sand soft enough to dig in and bury him. We were saddened, but angry with ourselves, and guilty that we hadn't chained him. I asked Asa if he would want to get another dog, but he didn't want that. I didn't either, and since that time neither of us has ever again owned a dog.

Chapter Ten

Even though television was in the surge of its youth, nobody I knew in Powder River owned one in January of 1958. I Love Lucy, Ed Sullivan's, Toast of the Town, Sid Caesar's, Show of Shows, along with Jackie Gleason's, Honeymooners, were all entertaining the nation and making it laugh, but for Asa and me, the radio remained the chief link with the outside world. We listened to the news and weather each morning and night. Even though he was not a rancher, he listened carefully for Stockman's Warnings, for so many of the PO clients were ranchers, and he worried about their welfare. The evening of January 28th, we began to listen closely, scooting to the edge of our chairs to hear the bulletins. Charles Starkweather was loose in Nebraska.

"We interrupt our musical presentation to bring you this special news bulletin. Law enforcement officials in Nebraska are on the lookout for nineteen-year-old, Charles Starkweather and his fourteen-year-old girlfriend, Caril Ann Fugate, who are suspected of killing Fugate's mother, stepfather and three-year-old half-sister in Lincoln sometime this morning.

Starkweather is described as five foot, five inches tall, weighing one hundred and forty pounds, with sandy red hair and wearing wire-rimmed glasses. Rural residents are advised to stay indoors and take caution when encountering strangers.

We repeat. Law enforcement officials in and around Lincoln, Nebraska are on the lookout for suspected killer, Charles Starkweather and his girlfriend, Caril Ann Fugate. The two are suspected of murdering the girl's family, all of Lincoln. Rural residents are being cautioned to stay indoors and report any unusual occurrences to local or state law enforcement authorities."

Asa immediately rose from his chair and went to the kitchen drawers where we kept our road maps. We spread the Nebraska map out on the kitchen table and pinpointed Lincoln. It seemed a long way off, tucked down in the southeast corner of the state.

"You think he'll come here?" I asked, my voice revealing my fear.

"Hard telling."

"It's a long way," I assured myself.

"No so far they couldn't drive it in a day," Asa countered, crumbling my hopes. With his finger he traced the mileage chart at the top of the map.

"About four hundred and twenty miles to Scottsbluff, and only another hundred and fifty or so to Casper."

"Wouldn't they go east toward Chicago, or up into Canada?" I asked hopefully.

"Hard to say. They might. You would think so, but it doesn't sound like a guy who'd killed his girlfriend's folks and a three-year-old child is in his right mind. No telling what a guy like that will do."

The bulletin was repeated twice that evening before we went to bed, but nothing new had been added, and we turned in wondering what the news would be by morning. By morning it was worse.

"Authorities in Lincoln, Nebraska have confirmed reports of more killings by mad killer, Charles Starkweather and his girlfriend, Caril Ann Fugate. In the early morning hours, Lancaster County sheriff's deputies discovered the bodies of a sixteen-year-old girl and her seventeen-year-old boyfriend in a culvert just outside Bennet, a community just south of Lincoln. Both young people had been shot with a shotgun. In addition, a seventy-year-old former employee of Starkweather's was found shot to death in his farmhouse not far from the death scene of the two younger victims.

Sheriff's deputies have alerted the State Police in surrounding states, and are cautioning all citizens to be on the alert for the two, young fugitives, who may be driving a blue, 1949 Ford, hot-rod roadster. That brings the death total to six in this horrible example of youth gone mad.

Charles Starkweather is described as five foot five inches tall, one hundred and forty pounds, light sandy-red hair, and wearing wire-rimmed glasses. Those who know him say he resembles movie star, James Dean.

Police report that Starkweather is armed with a .410 gauge shotgun and at least one handgun. He is extremely dangerous. The order has gone out to Nebraska law enforcement officers to shoot to kill. All rural residents are

The story was, of course, the talk of the day. On the school bus, and at school in the halls as well as in classrooms, the only subject was Starkweather. At lunch we voiced our fears that he might be headed our way. We hoped they could catch him by nightfall.

By the time I got out of school and boarded the bus for our return to Powder River, I was panicky with fear for Asa, and the news relayed on the bus ride only increased my fear.

One of the Natrona kids had a portable radio on the bus, and as we rode home on the last school day of January, the school bus was as silent as a church, which if you ever rode a school bus, you know to be a once in lifetime happening, as we were all straining to hear the latest bulletin.

"The savage butchery by suspected killer, Charles Starkweather, continued in Nebraska today. About mid-morning, Tom Windham, President of Central Steel Works in Lincoln, was found dead along with his wife and the couple's maid in Windham's home in Lincoln. Charles Starkweather's 1949 Ford was found in the Windham garage, and Windham's 1956 black Packard was reported missing.

That brings to nine, the number of people believed killed by young Starkweather. Authorities in Nebraska and surrounding states are warning..."

Folks in five states grew increasingly alarmed with the situation. Many armed themselves and sat in their living rooms waiting for Starkweather to show up. Citizens were deputized to help local authorities. Stories spread uncontrollably as if carried on the wind: *Starkweather had killed four children and their mother in Columbus. Two filling station attendants in Hastings were found bludgeoned to death. A ninety year old woman in Omaha was found shot in her home.* All rumors. None of them true. The truth was bad enough, nine dead, and Starkweather still at large.

Charles Starkweather and his girlfriend were sighted as far north as Norfolk, and as far south as Topeka, Kansas. They were reported to be in a grocery store in Council Bluffs at the same time a filling station attendant pumped gas for them at North Platte. He was sighted in four different states on the same day. It was as he could move faster than a speeding bullet.

Coming so soon on the heels of Asa's brush with death, the incidents had me spooked something awful. I couldn't get to Powder River fast enough. As soon as the bus dropped me off at Swede's, I ran west along the highway toward the PO, eager to get to Asa while he was still alive. Images of him lying crookedly on the Post Office floor, shirtfront soaked with blood, his arm sticking through the rungs of his overturned stool filled my mind. *I'm shot in the chest and I think I might die.* I burst through the front door of the PO on a dead run, sending it slamming into the wall like a gunshot.

"Asa!" I shouted, and frightened three customers and Asa as well, who, like everyone else knew that Starkweather was still on the loose, and probably thought he'd kicked in the door to gun them down. Assessing the situation immediately, Asa reassured everyone with a calm voice.

"It's okay, Matthew. We're all just fine. You folks know Matthew, my son. He's been a little alarmed about this Starkweather fella, what with me getting shot back in November."

I stood there as the beat of my heart began its slow descent to normal, the three customers staring at me, speechless.

"Whyn't you go on home now, Matthew. I'll be along about five-thirty. We can get dinner at the Tumble Inn if you want. Go ahead. It's all right. I'll see you later."

Feeling like a fool, I muttered an apology and backed out into the cold, January air. Instead of going directly home, I went to Swede's where I explained what had happened and worked for an hour, dropping wrenches, pinching my fingers and cursing until Swede sent me home early to get my bearings.

As I stepped into our house, I tried to calm myself. I knew that Asa was fine, and that I'd just been with Swede, and he too was alive. Yet, I couldn't help being afraid. I knew Lincoln wasn't all that far away, and hoped the police or the sheriff of some county along the way would get Starkweather long before he got to Wyoming. He might not even be headed in our direction, I told myself. Maybe he was still holed up around Lincoln, hiding in some farmer's barn or in an abandoned farm house out on the prairie somewhere. I prayed that he would be caught before he killed more people, and hoped he wouldn't get as far as Wyoming, and certainly not as far as Casper.

Still, when I felt the emptiness of the house, the first thing I did was load the .22. I even put a round in the chamber, and then sat in Asa's chair listening to the radio for the latest developments, the loaded rifle across my lap forgetting that I couldn't even shoot a horse or a dog to end their misery.

Shortly after five-thirty, when Asa came home and found me sitting armed in his chair, he was really concerned. He stood before me for a few moments, studying me, great worry on his face.

"That rifle's loaded, no doubt."

I nodded. "There's a round in the chamber," I confessed, a little sheepishly.

He reached out and lifted the rifle from my lap. He ejected the bullet and emptied the rest of the rounds, placing them on the table next to the radio. He leaned the rifle in the corner.

"Listen, Matthew," he said, sitting on the sofa across from me, leaning forward with his elbows on his knees.

"We can't go around being afraid for the rest of our lives. I know how you feel. I can feel the same way. A stranger will enter the PO and I'll think, 'Oh no! Not again.' But we can't live our lives that way. We got to get back to normal. You got to believe we'll be okay, that we'll always see one another again at the end of each day. You got to have enough faith in your God to know that he'll care for us."

"I had faith before, but Lydia left, you got shot, Lucky is dead and this crazy killer is headed our way."

"I know, but you got to believe anyway. If you can't do that, you'll never go to school in the fall. You'll never make a life of your own. I'm all right here. Nothing's going to happen. Now, let's go eat. I'm hungry. They'll probably have caught this guy by morning."

I knew Asa was right, and tried to calm myself, but by morning the news had worsened. Starkweather had been spotted first at Kimball, then at Scottsbluff. He was heading west. After breakfast as Asa left for work, I told him I was going to work with him at the PO, but he wouldn't let me.

"Ain't you workin for Swede?"

"I'll call him and tell him I can't come in."

"You'll do no such thing. Remember what I said last night. We can't run scared all of our lives. You got to work and I got to work. It's what we have to do. This whole thing will be over by nightfall, and if it ain't, it'll be over tomorrow."

After Asa left, I walked through the back door of Hyatt's General Store on the way to the filling station, only to find the store filled with armed ranchers huddled around the wood stove, coffee in one hand and a rifle or a shotgun in the other. A few wore holstered handguns at their belts. One wore a Bowie knife as well. He was a government hunter named Harold Mackey. He was a diminutive man, and the Bowie knife ran down his thigh to damned near his kneecap.

"Mornin Matthew," Hyatt said in greeting. The others nodded or spoke their greetings. Clive Svareland was there, as was the Frenchman, Louvet, who'd probably poisoned Lucky. It looked like a scene from, *Gunfight at the OK Corral.*

"We're waitin for Starkweather to show up," Clive said. "We're ready for him." It was like Clive to become the spokesman.

"What will you do if he gets here?" I asked naively.

"Shoot him," Clive said. "What else?"

But by noon that very day, Saturday, January 30, 1958, Starkweather and Caril Ann Fugate were captured just outside of Douglas, Wyoming, a mere sixty miles from Powder River, but not before they killed their tenth victim.

It turned out that a thirty-seven-year-old coffee salesman had pulled his car off the road, apparently to get some sleep. Starkweather and his girlfriend needed another change of cars, so pulled up behind the guy, climbed into his vehicle and shot him in the head with a .22 revolver.

At about the same time, an oil field worker, thinking there'd been an accident, stopped to help. When he approached the car, Starkweather pointed a rifle out the window of the car and said something like, "I'll kill you."

The oilfield worker grabbed the rifle, figuring if he were to live he'd have to fight. While they scuffled, a Wyoming State Patrol car showed up. As the patrolman ran toward the struggling men, Caril Ann Fugate leaped out of the car and threw herself into the patrolman's arms, screaming, "It's Charles Starkweather. He's going to kill me."

Meanwhile, Starkweather took off in the black Packard, and a wild chase followed, with speeds reaching nearly a hundred miles an hour. The State Patrol officer radioed for help, and roadblocks were set up, which Starkweather rammed through in a hail of bullets. He was struck in the neck and ear, and finally gave up without a fight. He was actually crying when they handcuffed him.

Sunday morning, Asa and I read every word in the Casper Morning Star and the Rocky Mountain News about the killer. It was the number one story in the region, and also got a lot of national press coverage.

I studied the photo of Starkweather standing insolently in front of a patrol car, bound by handcuffs and leg irons. He wore a denim shirt, jeans and wire rimmed glasses, just as the radio had described, and his unruly hair did make him look a little like James Dean.

The reports said his IQ was 86. He'd fought a lot in school, and once stabbed another boy. His stepfather once told others that Charles had the, "seed of madness," in him. When he was arrested, Starkweather told the officers he'd decided to become an outlaw, but didn't know it would be so hard.

The excitement of the Starkweather news didn't abate after his capture. For another week, newspapers and magazines editorialized on the situation. When we learned from Time and Newsweek that Starkweather had killed a filling station attendant two months before, a crime unsolved until he was captured, our interest increased.

We asked all the questions. How could a fourteen-year-old girl follow the lead of a crazy killer, and participate in the deaths of her family, including a three-year-old girl? And virtually no one believed her claim to be a kidnap victim who feared for her own life.

The news magazines had photos of the two killers. He looked wild, sullen, threatening. She looked ordinary, young and lost. What had attracted her to him?

His trial began in May and ended in June when he was found guilty and ordered to be executed. His lawyer filed an insanity plea, but the court wouldn't have any of it. It was an interesting point for me in my newfound interest in becoming a lawyer. All along, everybody said how crazy he was. They called him a madman, a mad-dog killer, and just plain nuts. Who else would do such a thing? Clearly, he was insane.

But because insanity was grounds for acquittal, nobody wanted him acquitted. Although he was crazy to do it at all, he wasn't so crazy that he didn't know what he was doing, therefore, he had to die. In March of 1959, just over a year after his shooting spree, Charles Starkweather was executed by the State of Nebraska.

Caril Ann Fugate, on the other hand, received a life sentence. The court didn't buy her story that she'd been held captive by her boyfriend. Her trial didn't even begin until October, and because of the time-lapse and the fact that she didn't seem a threat to society, she didn't die. It did appear that Starkweather had done all the shooting, but more importantly, the court was lenient on her because she was a girl.

In my thinking, and apparently in the thinking of most folks, a girl or a woman shouldn't be executed, except in cases of national security, which allowed the government to execute a woman named Ethel Rosenberg, along with her husband, Julius, in June of 1953 for selling atomic secrets to the Russians.

But Caril was only a girl-child of fourteen, led astray by the older, malevolent man. He died, she didn't. Justice and mercy were illustrated by their respective sentences. At the time it made sense to me, and I was not alone in my thinking.

I studied the case with great interest. Until that year I hadn't paid much attention to criminal matters, and hadn't ever given the death penalty one thought. But while reading the arguments offered by the western press, I had mixed thoughts about it. For although I felt Starkweather did deserve to die, it was pretty clear that his death would not deter any other killer from committing similar crimes. History bears that out. Someone is always crazy or angry enough to find good reasons to kill someone else. Men went mad, and periodically splashed the pavement with innocent blood, and although it was true that Charles Starkweather never again killed, his execution didn't keep others from wreaking havoc on their victims.

But as a youth of sixteen, fascinated with the power of the death penalty and the mercy of the court, I was pleased with the outcome. Starkweather had died, and deservedly so. Caril Ann would live to be released thirty years later and be given a new identity to live out her late years in anonymity.

Chapter Eleven

After the excitement that began at Thanksgiving and extended through January, February and March were a respite for Asa and me. We did little but go to work and school, and on weekends we read, took naps and walked through the countryside. We missed the dog, and of course, we still missed Lydia, but the ache was beginning to soften.

By late March we were all pretty tired of winter. The wind never quit, and it was far too cold. Asa wished for warm weather, for his chest and ribs hurt in the cold, something he never escaped. He looked forward to warm weather to soothe his pain, and he began to talk about moving to Nevada after I left for college in the fall.

I turned seventeen on March 17th, so to celebrate we drove into Casper to have dinner at the Townsend Hotel and take in a movie at the America Theater to see Glenn Ford and Jack Lemmon in a western called, *Cowboy*. Both Asa and I thought it was a fine movie. We also saw coming attractions of *The Bridge Over the River Kwai*, and since Asa loved WWII material, we planned to see it the next week. Though mild, it turned out to be a memorable birthday, the last one I'd celebrate while living in Powder

River, for by the next one I'd be away from home and on my own.

Spring Break was the first week of April, and Hetty and I decided to drive up to Thermopolis to swim at the Washaki Hot Springs. Asa let me take the pickup, and we struck out about nine o'clock.

It was a cold morning, just over thirty-four degrees, so we ran the heater which made the cab really cozy with the fan humming softly as it turned out the heat.

The drive was pleasant. We sighted jack rabbits, hawks and two, young coyotes along the way. I drove slowly, being in no hurry, but just enjoying the ride and Hetty's talk. We stopped in Shoshone at the Sagebrush Café for a cup of coffee and a piece of apple pie, and as we walked back to the truck, I asked her if she wanted to drive.

"Matthew, I can't drive. You know that. I don't even think they'd give me a license."

"I don't care about the license. You can drive. Come on. Drive for a while. Who'd know?"

"What if I run into something?"

"You won't. There's only sagebrush and greasewood."

She stood with her hand on the wall of the truck bed, looking at me while trying to decide, her hair permed softly around her face, her sunglasses reflecting my image. She was wearing a yellow, flowery western shirt, a pair of faded jeans, and cowboy boots. She smiled at me.

"Okay, but don't let me crash."

"You won't crash. Come on."

She walked around from behind the truck and slipped into the driver's seat. She adjusted the seat by sliding the bench forward a bit. I climbed in the other side while she fiddled with the rearview mirror. When she was settled, she took a deep breath and turned the ignition and put the truck in gear. She eased out onto the highway headed north to Thermopolis.

"Sit in the middle, Matthew, like all the kids do," she requested. "Just in case you have to grab the wheel."

I slid over next to her knowing full well that she just wanted me closer, for she drove her daddy's truck all over the ranch and never ran into anything that I ever knew. She just hadn't driven on the highway, is all, and just needed some experience to gain confidence.

The gear shift was on the floor in the center, so I couldn't sit too close to her, but from time to time as the road banked left or right, our thighs touched. It was as if we were going together. We could feel like that sometimes when no one else was around.

"You're weaving a little," I said. "Straighten it out."

"I'm not weaving," she objected, but sat up and got a better grip on the wheel.

"You sound like my father," she complained.

"Hmmm. I do a little, don't I?"

I left her alone after that. There was only an occasional car or truck on the road, and as we both knew, she drove well enough.

"Matthew, I have a present for you in my bag. Reach down there on the floor and get that envelope out of it. It's got your name on it."

"A present?" I asked. "What present? For what?"

"Oh, don't get excited. It's not much. Just get the envelope."

I reached down and pulled a manila envelope out of her bag. My name was written in Hetty's careful handwriting. I could tell it was a graduation announcement with a senior picture included.

"Go ahead. Open it."

"Keep your eyes on the road and speed it up a little, Hetty," I said a little embarrassed. "We want to get to Thermopolis by nightfall."

I slid my finger under the flap of the envelope and took out the announcement. It featured the Wyoming Mustang embossed in gold with black and orange letters reading, "Class of 58."

When I opened the announcement a wallet-sized photo dropped into my lap. I picked it up and studied it. It was a really nice picture of her, softly lighted and shadowed to help disguise the shape of her head. Her face was in profile, hiding the horse shoe shaped scar.

"Oh, Hetty, it's a great picture," I told her honestly. "Are you happy with it?"

"You know, Matthew, after my accident I felt I was ugly. For years I would look at the pictures my mother took in the years before I got trampled, and I would see this pretty little girl, and then I looked in the mirror at my scar and the shape of my head and I would just cry. My mother had to put all the old photos away for the longest time, but recently I can see that I'm not ugly. I just have scars, is all. I'm not pretty, I know, but I think I look okay. And that senior picture, Matthew, well it's just beautiful to me. I haven't looked that nice since the day before my accident. I know you shouldn't love your own picture, but I do. I just love it."

I didn't know what to say, so I turned the photo over and read what she'd written.

Matthew, my true friend. We've had such good times. I'll always remember our Junior/Senior prom, and all of August with you at the ranch. Stay the way you are.

Love,
Hetty.

"Thank you," I said, turning to her, watching her face as she drove, and seeing the deep beauty she'd always had within her.

"I have one for you too. It's home. I was going to wait until yearbooks came out, but I'll give it to you before we go back to school. Thank you, Hetty, it's really special."

"I don't want to drive anymore," she said softly. "I have something in my eye."

Tears filled her eyes and ran down her cheeks.

"Pull over. I'll drive."

She pulled off the road, put the truck in neutral and stepped out, leaving the driver's door open. I did the same from my side, and we walked around the back of the truck. She grabbed me and gave me a fierce hug. We clung to one another for just a moment, leaning against the tailgate, saying nothing. It was all I could do to keep from crying myself.

After I adjusted the seat and the mirror and we got rolling again, she surprised me for the second time when she said, "Matthew, I think I want to be a pastor?"

"What?" I reacted, looking over at her.

"Keep your eyes on the road, Matthew, you're weaving a little," she said, laughing.

I too laughed, hearing my own words.

"I thought you were going to teach math?" I asked.

"I was. I mean, I might do that too, but I don't want to now. I want to be a woman pastor."

"You can't be a woman pastor, Hetty. There are no woman pastors. You mean a missionary?"

"No, not a missionary, a woman minister. Why do women always have to be the Sunday school teachers and the missionaries? There must be women pastors somewhere. It's going to be the sixties soon, Matthew.

"It's like we're in the Dark Ages. I want to be a pastor in a small town like Riverton or Lander. I want to run the church, give sermons, serve communion, and not just read the Sunday school enrollment and count the money."

I was amazed at Hetty's revelation and fervor. I'd never heard of a woman being a pastor, never had given it any thought.

"What did your folks say?"

"I haven't told them yet. I'm afraid to tell Daddy. I think it will be better for me to go away to college first, then before I declare my major, I'll write to them."

"How will you be able to give sermons if you're even afraid of telling your father?" I asked.

"That's different. Besides, I won't be ministering to my father."

"What do you have to do to become one?"

"Well, you go to school for four years for your B.A. Then you go to a seminary, a divinity school."

"Oh, that'll be divine. Will you learn to make divinity?"

"Be serious, Matthew. This is important. God has been very good to me. I almost died the year of my accident. I could have had serious brain damage, but all that happened is that I lost some balance and my face is scarred. I've always been good in arithmetic. I got smarter at it as I grew older, and I haven't missed a problem in math since who knows when. I've been blessed by God, and I want to serve him by being a pastor, by leading his flock."

I could hear as she talked how important it was to her, and I hated to see her so excited about it because I didn't believe a woman could become one. I didn't even know what a divinity school was, and I was sure they wouldn't accept her anyway, her being a girl.

But as we drove she continued to talk, and I could see some real sense to it. Hetty was a walking miracle. Having been stepped on by a horse had transformed her into a math genius. Maybe she would have been a genius anyway. Who knows? But I could see her telling her story in front of a church congregation, a beam of light shining down on her through a high window, making a halo out of her softly permed hair. Certainly her sermons would be far better than a lot of sermons I'd heard. She'd probably make a good minister. I drove on silently, pondering the mysterious twists life takes so suddenly.

We got to Thermopolis about eleven thirty and decided to swim before eating lunch. I was a little embarrassed to have Hetty see me in my bathing trunks. It made me feel naked and vulnerable, but I could see that she felt the same, though I thought she looked good in her one-piece suit. She was still thin, but her breasts had filled out and her hips as well. She was pale, but then so was I. To keep our embarrassment down we spent all of our time up to our necks in the water. The air was still cold, so the hot springs felt good. We stayed in too long, of course, and felt all weak and loop legged by the time we got out.

Afterwards we walked over to a nearby A&W and ordered burgers, fries and malts to go. We ate in the truck with the motor running and the radio playing, and the inside of the cab smelled like onions and grease.

After lunch we walked along the wooden boardwalks that wound through the hot springs. We'd read stories every summer of kids falling into the deep pools there and at Yellowstone National Park, and being severely burned, sometimes boiled to death. So we were conscious of it and held one another's hand tightly the whole time.

Our drive back was slow and easy. We started back about four-thirty or so, and chattered about school, being lawyers and ministers, and how we were going to miss the Powder River gang.

We also talked about Hetty's college scholarship possibilities. She was most interested in the University of California at Berkeley. I was just hoping to start at Casper College and maybe later I could scholarship at the University of Wyoming at Laramie.

When we got home, we were hungry again, and not wanting the day to end, we ate at the Tumble Inn, drawing looks from the waitresses and the adults who knew us. They wanted us to be in love, which we weren't, but we did love one another. Hetty loved the attention though, and I didn't mind, it being generally harmless and based only on genuine affection and the inevitable small-town need for gossip.

Before I took her home, we went up to my place where Hetty and Asa talked while I wrote on the back of my senior picture and gave it to her.

She didn't read what I wrote until I was driving out to her ranch, and it made her cry again.

May began with that great electrical charge all high school seniors feel when they know graduation is just around the corner. It would be a busy month. Yearbooks would be out June 6th, two days before the prom, and graduation would take place outside in the football stadium on the 15th of June, weather permitting. It was what every class hoped for, but it seldom happened. Wyoming weather had a mind of its own, and was always unpredictable. If it wasn't freezing, it would be hot and blowing forty miles an hour. Still, we prayed for a calm evening, so we would be one of the few classes to have our ceremony outdoors.

Although I was pleased to have given out my senior pictures, especially the one to Hetty, I wasn't sure I liked them. Though Lydia and Asa carried on proudly, I thought they made me look too clean, handsome in a way I wasn't. In the photo I had no blemishes, no loose strands of hair or anything, and my smile was wider than my natural smile, and showed too many teeth. My mother told me I looked like Asa when he was young, but I couldn't see it.

I hadn't been able to decide about the prom and thought I just as well ask Hetty again. She was such a safe date. We understood one another, and neither of us held any expectations. Still, the thought of a new girl did appeal to me, so I thought I'd wait and think on it a bit more, believing that any senior girl who hadn't been asked would accept a late invitation. The day yearbooks were distributed we spent the entire day signing them. *Tradition*, they called it, but we all knew teachers were tired of teaching, just as we were tired of learning.

The ride home to Powder River was another rare, fairly quiet time on the bus, as we were all busy signing and reading annuals. Hetty reserved a page for me, as I did for her, and we sat side-by-side writing as neatly as the swaying bus would allow. The next day would be our first graduation rehearsal. We were alive with the knowledge that in a few weeks, it would all be over. We'd be free of all responsibilities.

We deluded ourselves, of course. It wouldn't all be over. It would be just the beginning. Within a week after graduation, most of us would be working full time. One or two would get married within the month. Some would join the army. In the fall many of us would be starting college, and within a year, some would have babies. Five years would bring the first divorce; and one or two of us would die in the course of the summer, drowning in a drainage ditch or being crushed by a ranch truck. Ranch work took lives every summer. It was part of life around Powder River.

Shortly after six the next Monday morning, Asa and I were listening to the radio while getting ready for work and school, when the phone rang. Asa answered it. I was shaving, a task I loved doing four days a week. It was the visible sign of my manhood, that mysterious country I had begun to move into the past year.

I heard Asa's soft voice only a few times during his conversation. I was splashing water over my face to remove the soap when I looked up and saw his image in the mirror, standing in the bathroom doorway, his face pale and drawn, and I thought immediately that Lydia had died.

"What? Is it Lydia?" I asked fearfully.

"Hetty's dead," he whispered. "She died in her sleep. Her mother found her when she went to wake her."

I felt a quick stab in my chest, felt my breath shorten. I grabbed Asa and sobbed once into his shirt as he wrapped his arms around me and held me tightly. Then I stepped away from him and reached for a hand towel to dry the soapy water and the tears from my face.

"Today's the first graduation rehearsal."

"Yes."

"What happened?"

"They don't know. She just died in her sleep, is all."

"I want to go see her," I said, brushing past him. "I have to see her."

"She's dead," Asa said, following me into my bedroom.

"I know she's dead," I shouted. "But I've got to see her."

"We'll both go." Asa nodded. "They're going to need some help out there."

We drove in silence, my tears finished temporarily, my pain turning to anger at the unfairness of life. Hetty dead before her graduation, before she could use either of her scholarships, and before she realized the dream of being a pastor.

The Places, standing on the porch, watched us drive up. Mrs. Place stood red-eyed, tightly clutching a damp handkerchief, her fist pressed against her mouth. Her husband stood behind her, tears in his eyes, his lip quivering in a forced smile as he tried to be strong. He looked smaller than I'd ever seen him, so diminished that it was hard to believe he'd held Whitey Carlson up against the wall of the general store the day I took my beating. We all hugged and held one another on the porch, reluctant to go inside.

"May I see her?" I asked.

Mrs. Place took my hand and led me into Hetty's room, leaving me alone, closing the door behind me. I sat in a hard-backed chair against the wall across from Hetty's bed and looked at her.

She lay on her side, the scars of her face hidden against the pillow. Her hair was bunched and tight, her right hand curled up slightly alongside her face. She wore silky, wine-colored pajamas with white piping. Her thick glasses lay on the nightstand next to her bed, and her yearbook lay on the floor with a pen tucked between the pages.

She was in the pose of sleep, but she didn't look asleep. She looked dead. The living quality, the essence that was Hetty, was gone. I didn't want to believe what I was seeing.

I reached out and touched her face. It was cool, and I kept my hand there as if to transfer some of my life's warmth to her. I wanted to deny the truth, wanted to know that she really was asleep and would awaken when she was all slept out. I wanted to bring her back to life, to give her again the breath she had breathed the day before. I had helped save Asa be giving him my blood, and wanted badly to save Hetty too.

So I sat with my warm hand on her cheek until I couldn't see very well because of my tears, and when I couldn't stand it any longer I walked out of her room, out through their living room and off the porch to the road Hetty and I had walked August past, the day we found and killed the rattlesnake.

I went to school. I wanted to be the one who cleaned out her locker, the one who brought all of her stuff back home to her folks. I wanted too, to be at the graduation rehearsal for her, believing somehow that if I went through it so soon after she'd died that her spirit would still be in touch with me before it got too far away, and she would know and feel what I felt at the rehearsal.

I had couple of bad minutes when the senior class adviser announced to the class in the assembly hall that Hetty had died. I didn't think I was going to make it, but Ernie, Adriana and Tom Svareland were sitting around me, and among us we shared a great bond. I knew it was just as difficult for them as it was for me, and so we supported one another until the moment passed.

Hetty's funeral service was held at the Powder River church five days after she died. It would have been sooner, but they had to do an autopsy to determine the cause of death, which turned out to be an aneurysm in her brain.

Also, her daddy wanted her buried on his ranch, which was illegal, but his lawyer figured out that if he set aside a portion of his land as a cemetery and registered it as such with Natrona County, he could do it. So he registered a half-acre behind his house, and that's where she was buried. He and Mrs. Place were buried there too, eventually, because he wrote into the papers that whoever owned the land over the next ninety-nine years must keep the cemetery intact. The place has sold twice over since then, and the folks on the ranch today still maintain Place's Cemetery. If I'm around, I try to put flowers on their graves on Memorial Day.

The Powder River church was packed with flowers and people. Rows of chairs were set up outside facing the door, and they too were filled. Inside it was almost too close to breathe. Almost everybody who had lived in Powder River at any time the Places had lived there, attended. Whitey Carlson was there alone. Lydia drove out to be with Asa and me, making us a family one more time. I helped to bear the pall, along with Tom Svareland, Ernie Clasp and three of the townsmen.

It was easier for me at the gravesite than in the confines of the church. The open spaces comforted me, knowing that Hetty was buried on her own land, and that she wouldn't be in a cemetery among people she didn't know. Not that it makes any difference, really, but at the time it seemed the only place she should have been buried.

I didn't mind missing the prom. It seemed there was a reason I couldn't decide whom to ask. I'd attended the prom I was meant to attend.

We did not graduate outdoors, and I was pleased that we didn't get the opportunity Hetty missed. The weather grew unseasonably cold, with morning frosts and winds reminiscent of March. We graduated in the high school auditorium amongst the almost universal sounds and sights of all high school graduations: applause, flashbulbs, cowbells ringing out in pride.

Afterwards, Lydia, Asa and I went to the Townsend Hotel for dinner. Lydia would have preferred the Gladstone, but the Townsend was neutral ground. I sat facing the window and the street beyond, aware of her name on the marquee across the street.

Neither of them had given me a gift, and I thought in the turmoil of Hetty's death they'd forgotten and would get around to it later. But after dinner we drove my mother back to her apartment, and there parked in front was a pink and white, 1950 Pontiac with a sign on the windshield which read, "Congratulations, Matthew!"

"I'm sorry about the pink," Asa apologized. "We can paint it. It was a good buy."

Graduation summer I worked for Mr. Place driving pickup, hauling gear from one end of the ranch to the other, making runs to Casper and delivering loaned and borrowed tools. Ranchers always loaned and borrowed something, often making no distinction between the two words. "Borrow me that post hole digger of yours next Saturday," someone would say, and it would be loaned to him.

In many ways, it was a painful summer, since it was somewhat of a repeat of the summer before with Hetty. During solitary times I sat at Hetty's grave talking with her silently, or aloud when I was sure no one was within earshot. And once in a while as I walked out alone over the prairie, the wind would carry the faint sound of Hetty's voice to me. I would stop and shade my eyes against the sun, searching, knowing full well that she was gone.

During that summer, I realized that much of what we have in life, if not everything, is only loaned and borrowed. Hetty's life had been loaned to me, and to her parents; and in return, I loaned her my attention, my companionship, my love. We shared what we borrowed without selfishness, without the thought of repayment. When she died the loan became due, payment made, and despite the almost unbearable pain, I was the richer for it.

By summer's end, I began to make some sense of it, and the idea of loaning and borrowing helped. I continued to be troubled, however, by Lydia's decision to leave us the year before. Even on loan, she should have been in our home longer. Hetty's death was one thing, but Lydia's departure before I was grown and moved away seemed a greater debt to be paid, which has, in effect, remained unpaid. And as I matured, I felt that Asa's loss was more costly than mine, for Lydia remained my mother, but not so Asa's wife.

Now long after college graduation, in my work as a lawyer, seeking justice for my clients and peace for myself, I drive Wyoming highways, crisscrossing the state taking depositions, trying cases, counseling and trying to listen to the right voices. The wind whips snow or sand over my windshield, and I see Hetty and Tom, Adriana and Ernie at the bus stop, or walking down the road from Place's.

As I swing through Powder River, the town itself is only half what it was when I lived there. All the buildings along the south side of the Highway have been moved or bulldozed away. The Tumble Inn has become a derelict, waiting for the bulldozer to put it out of its misery, the Legion Hall moved to Waltman. Hyatt's store too is gone, Swede's Shell Station boarded up along with the motel cabins he rented out across the road, and our white frame house is no longer there. I find no reason to stop.

The year of my mother's leaving, of my seduction, of Asa's wounding and of Hetty's death was the year of my passage. Throughout my college career, when a literature professor spoke of the rite of passage as a literary theme, I understood exactly what he meant, and I know too I have become the man I am, in great part, because of the events that occurred in Powder River in 1957.

***